Woodsman Werebear

(Saw Bears, Book 6)

T. S. JOYCE

Woodsman Werebear

ISBN-13: 978-1537787411
ISBN-10: 1537787411
Copyright © 2015, T. S. Joyce
First electronic publication: July 2015

T. S. Joyce
www.tsjoyce.com

NOTE FROM THE AUTHOR:
This book is a work of fiction. The names, characters, places, and incidents are products of the writer's imagination or have been used fictitiously and are not to be construed as real. Any resemblance to persons, living or dead, actual events, locale or organizations is entirely coincidental. The author does not have any control over and does not assume any responsibility for third-party websites or their content.

Published in the United States of America

First digital publication: July 2015
First print publication: September 2016

Editing: Corinne DeMaagd

ONE

It came to Riley's attention two years too late she had terrible taste and worse luck in men.

Another knock pounded so hard against the doorframe, the vibration rattled a picture frame off the wall and shattered the glass across her tile floor. A pathetic whimper clawed its way up the back of her throat. With shaking hands, she threw another handful of clothes into the duffle bag on her bed

"Riley, let me the fuck in! That's my baby, too!"

"No, she's not! I've already explained that to you," Riley screamed. "She isn't yours, and she isn't mine."

"The baby is a she?" His voice dipped to a calmer, saner tone. "I don't care that you cheated when I was locked up, baby. I don't even care that you testified against me."

Bullshit. She wouldn't be fooled by Seamus Teague. Not this time. That man had the devil in him, and she was smarter now than when she'd been with him before.

"I have a restraining order, Seamus," she called out. "I'm calling the police." Again.

"No, you ain't. You already done called 'em twice tonight, and I'm betting they told you to give it a rest last time they paid you a visit. Let me in, baby. Come on." A soft, muffled sound filled the air, as if he was petting the door.

He was right, damn his cunning. She'd felt watched all night and could've sworn his best friend Jeremy's Toyota was parked in front of her apartment, but when the police had come out both times, Seamus was in the wind.

And now he was going to kill her.

The baby rolled inside the swell of her stomach. "Shhh," Riley cooed, rubbing her hand over her taut middle. "I won't let anything happen to you."

A fierce protectiveness washed over her as she straightened her spine and glared at the door. She wouldn't be one of his victims, and she sure as shit wasn't going to let this little angel be tainted by his poisonous love.

When she looked around her apartment, at the furniture she'd picked out and the dishes waiting in the clear glass cupboards her mom had gifted her when she'd moved in, a deep ache bloomed inside of her. She'd had a good life here until Seamus had messed everything up. The court, too, since they'd been the ones to make his sentence light enough that he was here, threatening her, rather than rotting away in prison as he deserved.

She wiped her sweating palms on her jeans and slid the strap of her duffle bag over her shoulder. Breath hitching and throat clogging with fear, she picked up a handgun she'd bought and learned how to use when she'd found out what a monster Seamus was.

All she had to do was make it out the main door where her friend April was waiting to drive her to the bus station. If she left now, she'd make one of the last buses leaving for the night, and Seamus would be delayed searching for her.

Checking the safety on her weapon, she padded to the door and threw it open wide.

Aiming the gun, she gritted out, "Get the fuck out of my way, or I'll pull this trigger and dance on your fucking carcass."

Seamus's dark, empty eyes widened as if he was surprised—which was impossible because Seamus Teague didn't feel emotions, the cold-blooded snake. He lurched forward, grip barely missing her weapon, but she expected nothing less from him and jerked it out of his way, cocking the gun at the same time.

The crack of metal on metal stopped him, and slowly, he lifted his hands in surrender. A show, surely, because Seamus had never given up on anything as long as she'd known him. Riley gripped the handle harder to ease the tremble in her fingers, then twitched the gun impatiently. "I said move."

"Let's just discuss this like civilized people. That baby might not be blood related to me, but we're a family—"

"Move!" she screamed, the heat of fury blasting up her neck.

His snake-eyes narrowed, but he moved by

inches, creating enough room in the doorway for her to get by.

Never turn your back on a predator. She backed down the hallway, weapon trained on the place where Seamus's heart should've been, if he had one.

His lip curled up in a snarl as he watched her leave. "It don't matter where you go, baby. And that restraining order don't mean shit to me. I'll find you no matter how long it takes to hunt you down. You got my baby in you now—my family."

"I told you," she murmured, swallowing a sob. "She ain't yours, and she ain't mine."

Her back hit the swinging exit door, so she turned and bolted for April's white Maxima parked right off the curb. Her friend had already thrown open the passenger's side door, bless her intuition.

Scream lodged in her throat, Riley slid into the car and shut the door as fast as she could before April peeled out of the parking lot.

When she looked behind her, Seamus was standing by the door, watching her leave with such hatred in his face, he looked like the monster he was inside. Twin tears rolled down her cheeks as she faced the front again. She had to stop doing that—

9

looking back.

Looking back had stunted her ability to lead a better life when he'd been locked up.

Looking back had thrown her life into a nightmare.

Looking back had kept her from healing from the horror she'd witnessed.

Riley nodded distractedly when April asked if she was all right.

She would be. Had to be.

Riley rubbed the tight swell of her belly and made another silent oath to protect the child she'd worked so hard to grow.

She'd talked on the phone to the biological parents of the baby she'd agreed to be a surrogate for, but this was the first time she would meet them in person.

And she sure as hell hoped Diem and Bruiser Keller were ready for the trouble that would be tailing her.

TWO

The sound of cracking bone was deafening as the man's fist connected with Drew's nose. Iron trickled into his mouth as pain seared through his face. The contender's eyes blazed an eerie green, and Drew laughed and spat crimson onto the stained plywood floor. Fuckin' shifter. He should've known.

Haydan was yelling his name from the roaring crowd in the dingy warehouse, but Drew ignored him. Haydan followed him around everywhere lately, worried over him like a mother hen. Drew placed his fingers on either side of his nose and jerked it straight before the bones healed crooked. Shifter

11

healing was a blessing and a curse.

Straightening his spine, Drew pulled his wrapped fists up to defend his face and circled his opponent slowly. The ref had introduced the goliath as Kong. Nicely done. Drew bet the old muscled-up bruiser was a King Kong with a face-pummeling right hook like his. Good. At least a gorilla shifter would give him a good fight. Thrashing cocky humans had grown old.

Sweat trickled down his bare shoulders as Drew ducked Kong's oversize fist. Drew leered at him as he pulled back just out of reach of his swing, then he blasted the gorilla in the ribs, once, twice, and then a crack on the third fast hit. Kong was strong, but quick he was not.

Drew's inner bear roared for revenge, dumping adrenaline into his system. Fuck, he had to keep the animal inside his skin. If he showed the crowd what he really was, Tagan would have his hide as a bearskin rug for his kid to play on. His alpha had set down a no-getting-caught order until he decided if the Ashe Crew was going to come out to the public or not.

Gritting his teeth, Drew took a hit to his middle

for the chance to get close to Kong's injured left side. He worked the cracked ribs, letting his mind go, living on instinct: ducking, dodging, hit, hit, swerve and circle back. Kong's knuckles were relentless, but so were Drew's, and a grizzly and a gorilla were a good match.

The crowd went mad, cheering and screaming their monikers.

"Kong, Kong, Kong!"

"Beast, Beast, Beast!"

This mob only applauded for blood, and he and Kong were staining the arena.

The fight dragged on until every inch of Drew's skin ached. Until his muscles tired and his knuckles were swollen and bloody. Until his arms felt like they were a hundred pounds. Until Kong's face wept red, and the sneer slipped from his mangled lips. The gorilla shifter's left side was purple, and he favored it. Drew huffed a laugh.

He had him.

All he had to do was stay conscious longer than Kong.

Haydan was yelling his name again, but he could piss off. Drew already knew what he'd say. *Your eyes, man. Hide your eyes.*

Yeah, they were probably glowing like shards of hardened ice right now, but fuck it all. He wasn't in a position to slip on a pair of sunglasses—not when he was this close to winning the match.

Drew charged. His fists connected with Kong's side as he wore out every combination his bleary mind could conjure. Kong's fists were brutal, pounding against him as he spent the last of his energy. He grunted when Kong landed a solid fist against Drew's jaw, snapping his head back, but he wasn't made of glass, and he was right back in there. Ribs, ribs, push off and *boom!* Drew's fist connected with Kong's jaw. Blood and sweat flung from his opponents damp hair on contact, and the behemoth hit the ground like a sack of bricks.

One of Drew's eyes was swollen shut, and his arms were heavy, as if they'd been made from cement, but he mustered the energy to give the crowd a bloody smile. The referee lifted his arm, declared him the winner, then pushed him toward Haydan, who looked disappointed.

But worse than the look of utter disappointment was the fact that his alpha, Tagan, was now standing beside Haydan. Shit.

A pair of jacked-up titans dragged Kong off the floor, smearing red across the dingy arena. Probably his crew.

Drew sauntered over to Tagan and Haydan, but neither of them were talking now, and both of them smelled like fur.

Judge, a squirrely man with two front teeth missing and shifty eyes, handed him a wad of fives and ones. "Good fight," he said, smacking Drew on the shoulder and drawing a wince from him. "See you next week."

"Yeah, thanks. See you next week."

Tagan yanked the cash from his hand, counted it quickly, and shoved it into his chest. "A hundred dollars?" he said too low for the humans around them to hear. Drew, however, could hear him just fine. He could also hear the snarl that tainted the words. "A hundred dollars to risk outing us? That's all it takes for you now?"

Drew jerked the money from his alpha's grasp and shoved it in his pocket. "A hundred dollars because I need the money, and until logging season starts up, I have to do what I have to do."

Drew shoved past him and Haydan and made his way through the crowd toward the exit. The cheering, jeering mob was focused on the next fight, two humans already smashing each other up, but without half the force of Drew's fight. He'd earned this hundred dollars tonight. His fights drew the crowds, and Judge always invited him back. Saturday evenings were always good for a quick wad of cash.

"Logging season starts in less than a week, Drew," Tagan gritted out from behind him. "You couldn't wait a few days to start making legit income?"

Drew threw open the dilapidated exit door and strode across the gravel parking lot toward his old beater Ford pickup. "Come on, man. How long are you gonna bust my balls, huh? Everyone has a side-job in the off-season."

"Yeah, but none of the Ashe Crew takes jobs that threaten to expose us, Drew. None of us but you. I've told you to stop coming here—"

"Tagan—"

"I don't want to fuckin' hear it!" his alpha said with such force, Drew halted and the hairs on the back of his neck rose. Tagan came around the front of him and looked him square in the eye. "No more coming here. Season is starting, and until I decide whether or not we're coming out to the public like the Breck Crew did, you'll lay low and not force my hand. Drew..." Tagan's voice softened. "I'm sorry about your mom—"

"Don't," Drew ground out, closing his eyes and banishing the memories. "Don't talk about her."

"Someone has to, man. You aren't. You aren't dealing with it at all. You're just..." Tagan hooked his hands on his hips, bright blue eyes arcing toward the old barn they'd just come from. He shook his head. "Your bender needs to stop before you put us all in jeopardy. Control your bear, get your shit together, and come back to us. We don't know this Drew."

Drew huffed in disgust, but he got what Tagan was saying. He didn't recognize himself right now either.

Tagan sighed and gave him the order. "You won't come out here again. You're done fighting until I say otherwise. Go home, Drew." He turned on his heel and strode off toward his truck, Haydan following without a backward glance.

They didn't get it. Didn't understand any of this.

They should be celebrating his fights.

When he fought, there was pain. There was burning and aching.

At least when he fought, he felt.

And if Tagan knew what was really going on with Drew's bear, he'd be celebrating tiny victories right along with him, not banning him from the one thing that kept him sane.

****

Riley stuck her thumb out again, but the old clunker truck passed right on by without even slowing. She'd blame it on the driver for being a dick, but mostly, she sucked at hitchhiking. It was probably the potato sack of a trench coat she was wearing to conceal her pregnancy and her hideous hacked-up hair she'd cut in a hotel bathroom mirror to go incognito. It looked so easy when women did it on television, but she looked like a four-year-old had gone to town on her locks with a pair of those safety scissors from preschool.

And then the taxi driver had dumped her off on the mountain road with no explanation other than "the woods here are haunted, and this is as far as I'm willing to go."

Great. She totally believed in ghosts. Plus, she had no idea how much farther away Damon Daye's house was, and eventually it was going to get dark out here. So far, she'd seen no signs, only endless evergreens, some boulders, a mound of unidentifiable roadkill that had made her morning sickness come back with a vengeance, and miles of pothole-riddled asphalt. And haunted woods.

Up ahead, a strange sound echoed off the trees, and the truck slowed and pulled over to the side. She perked up, readjusted the strap of her duffel bag, and marched double time toward it, but alas, no, the truck had a flat. The driver wasn't stopping to give her a ride.

That's what he got for ignoring her sad attempt at hitchhiking. "Karma's a bitch," she muttered as she slowed her speed back down to meandering waddle.

When the driver emerged from his ride, her eyes nearly popped out of her face. The man was probably in his late twenties with a long, lithe stride as he jogged around the back of his truck. The evening sunlight threw gold highlights into his blond, shoulder-length hair. He ducked just before she got to take in his face, but a white T-shirt clung tightly to his muscular shoulders and hole-riddled jeans hung just right around his tapered waist.

Riley pursed her lips against the hormone surge that flushed heat through her body. A vision of her splaying her hands against his truck and bending over as he pummeled her from behind made her gasp and draw up short. She didn't even know the man, nor had she seen his face or talked to him at all. He wasn't even nice if his ignoring her completely was anything to go by, and his truck was a rust bucket. Not like she could judge since she didn't own a car, but it screamed he wasn't relationship material if he couldn't even take care of his truck, and *oh my gosh, why am I thinking about a relationship with this stranger?*

The word "fuck" echoed across the clearing as he kicked his tire and ran his hands through his hair, then flung them forward. He cast her a narrow-eyed glance as she approached, then froze fast, as if he'd been electrocuted. "You aren't a dude."

She gave him a humorless smile. "Nope. Definitely not a dude."

"You're not a Boarlander?"

His face was smeared with something. Dirt?

Grease? "What's a Boarlander?"

"You're in Boarlander territory. Why?" he asked, sauntering toward her, his gait graceful compared to her shuffle.

"I don't know what you're talking about or what you're asking," she murmured tiredly. "And I'm super bad at riddles, had a crap couple of days, and the only possible ride I've seen on this road ignored me, then called me a dude."

"Well, your hair confused me, and I only saw you from the back."

"We can't all look like Fabio," she deadpanned, coming to a stop in front of him and arching her neck back to take in his full height. Holy hell balls, he was tall. His eyes were a piercing blue, all surrounded by that...mud?

"Ha," he huffed out. "That's what my crew calls me, too."

"Your crew."

The man's nostrils flared, and he frowned. "What are you doing way out here?" Looking around pointedly, he said, "This ain't exactly a good spot to vacation."

"Oh, the hitchhiking gave me away as a tourist,

21

did it?"

"Dead giveaway."

Riley liked the easy way in which he bantered. Oh, he was still mad about his flat tire, but at least he could plaster on a smile and talk cordially, and right now, as tired as she was, she was going to say that spoke well of him.

"Want me to change that for you?" she asked.

His gold brows lifted high, and a small smile ghosted his lips. "You're offering to change my flat?"

Riley snorted and pressed her palms against her aching back. "No, I was joking. I will, however, sit over there by that tree and watch you change your flat while cheering you on, and then I will graciously accept a ride from you when you are through." She meandered off through the dry, early autumn grass and called over her shoulder, "I'm Riley Miller, by the way."

"Drew Hudson," the man said in a troubled tone. "Are you hurt?"

"No, why?"

"Because you're walking funny."

"You sure know how to compliment a dude-lady."

"No, I mean... Sorry. Forget it. Give me twenty minutes to change the tire, and I'll give you that ride."

"Go, Drew, go," she said, waving her fists half-heartedly in the air and fulfilling her promise to cheer him on.

THREE

Riley Miller. Drew liked her name. It suited her no-nonsense attitude and relaxed demeanor. She dressed like a hobo, clutched an oversize duffle bag in front of her like a shield, and her hair looked like she'd cut it herself, but her face...damn. Riley was a stunner.

Dark hair, dark lashes, and an olive complexion that said she had something exotic in her bloodline. Pacific Islander or native Hawaiian, perhaps. She certainly didn't look like the usual fare of townies down in Saratoga, and he'd bet his favorite pair of work boots she wasn't from around here. It was her eyes that had held him stunned when he'd turned toward her. They were wide, like a wood sprite's, and slightly slanted, and the color was a light brown-green he'd never seen on a human before.

And more curious than anything was the way his bear had stopped bitching the moment Drew locked eyes with the strange woman. In fact, his inner monster had seemed just as rocked by this little force of nature as Drew had been.

He cast a quick glance over at her as he loosened the spare tire from beneath his truck bed. She sat down under a stately pine tree, clutching her duffle to her stomach. With a sigh, she leaned back against the bark and offered him a smile. The expression didn't reach her eyes, though, not like it had a minute ago, and it struck him how much of their conversation had been an act for her. She looked exhausted now.

Worry niggled at him. He should feed her or…something. No. He wanted to donkey kick his instincts. She wasn't his to protect or coddle. She was a stranger, and as soon as he dropped her off to wherever she was going, he'd never see her again.

A soft growl rattled his throat at the thought of his limited time with Riley, but it was just his bear shifting his mind to anywhere other than Mom. Drew almost laughed. It was so fucking obvious. Tagan had banned him from fighting, and now his bear was desperate for something else to put his thoughts on. And he'd chosen a homeless ruffian with a questionable taste in haircuts and a fondness for baggy clothing.

That's all this was. Nothing more.

That matter solved, Drew jerked the spare tire out of its cradle and carried it to the front right where his other one was shredded.

"You're super strong," Riley observed.

Oh right, shit. "The tire is really light is all."

"I actually know a lot about cars. My dad was a mechanic, and he used to drag me to his shop when I was out for the summers. He put me to work on the payroll as soon as it was legal. No tires are weightless like you just made it look." There was a frown in her voice, as if she was trying to work something out in her mind. "Must be those big muscles. Are you a gym rat?"

Drew snorted. They did have a makeshift gym under an awning at the trailer park, but he didn't get his physique from there. And why was he blushing?

"I'm a lumberjack, not a gym rat."

"You're a lumberjack?"

When he stopped twisting the wrench on a particularly stubborn lug nut long enough to look over his shoulder, she had her head canted and her eyes narrowed. "I've never met a lumberjack before. I always imagined they wore more flannel and walked around with an ax slung over their shoulder. And maybe followed around by a blue bull."

"Oh, she's got Paul Bunyan jokes. No flannel until wintertime when it's colder than ice up in these mountains. I do have an ax in the bed of my pickup along with a bunch of other tools I randomly need, and no blue bull, though there is a little pygmy goat named Bo up where I live that follows me around and head-butts me in the shins whenever I'm not paying attention. He's a bit of an asshole."

"Aw, just a little goat against a big old mountain man," she crooned with a pouty lip he suddenly wanted to bite. "Maybe you're the asshole, and he is just reminding you." Her stifled smile and dancing eyes told him she wasn't serious.

She sure was a sassy little thing. And a beautiful distraction.

Hiding his amused grin, he went back to unscrewing the lug nuts on the rim of the ruined tire. "You know, I heard you say 'Karma's a bitch' earlier. Was that you saying my flat tire happened because I didn't offer you a ride?"

"Maybe. And how did you hear that? I was way over there."

Crap. "Uh, your voice carries out here. Are you a city slicker?"

"Yes, I am. I think this is the first time I've seen a pine tree besides the ones you can buy at a tree lot during the holidays."

"You like the views out here?" Why did her answer matter so much? He wanted her to like his territory. *Distraction, she is a distraction.*

"This country is the most beautiful place I've ever seen. Even the air smells clean."

The honest notes in her voice made him look at her again to see if her eyes had taken on the same dreamy quality her words had. To his disappointment, she was looking down at her duffle bag in her lap, though, hiding that gorgeous eye color from him.

"Riley? What are you doin' out here?"

With a slow inhalation of breath, she looked at him, leveling him with those beautiful eyes. "Running."

"From what?"

Sadness washed over her face as she shook her head.

"Okay, then what are you running to?"

Riley licked her full lips and shook her head again.

Frustrated at the pile of secrets she was obviously protecting, he tried a different angle. "Can you at least tell me where I'm taking you?"

The zip of her duffle bag was loud in the quiet of the mid-afternoon woods. She pulled out a folded piece of paper. "Ten-twelve Fleece Creek Way. I'm supposed to meet a man named Damon Daye in a week. I'm a little early."

The oxygen huffed from Drew's lungs as he froze. He must've heard her wrong. "Wait, what? You're going to Damon Daye's house?" Billionaire Lair was a better term for the mansion the old dragon had built into the side of a mountain. Whatever it was called, it was no place for a human. "What business do you have with him?"

"Do you know Mr. Daye?"

"Yeah." And he ate people who fucked with shifters. Ate. Them. "He isn't that friendly toward trespassers."

"Well, I wouldn't be trespassing since he invited me."

Drew looked at the beautiful woman in a new light now. Maybe she was to be Damon's claim. The ancient shifter had to be getting lonely for a mate. It had been a while since his last one had died. That was the trade-off for immortality. Everyone passed on while Damon stayed the same. Drew stood and clenched his fists at his side. If he thought a gorilla shifter was a good fight, well, battling a dragon for this little human would bring down entire forests. *No.* Drew closed his eyes and swallowed hard against the influx of bear's murderous thoughts. He wasn't fighting anyone for anyone. Damon was an ally. Hell, over the past year and a half, he'd been a friend to Drew and the rest of the Ashe Crew. If Damon wanted to court Riley, so be it. That wasn't any skin off his neck.

"Are you okay?" Riley asked from right in front of him. "You're shaking."

Drew shook his head, feeling drunk and unbalanced with her so close. He took a step back out of self-preservation. "Yeah, I'm fine. I've just had a shit day."

"I can tell. You have mud all over your face." Riley was staring at him, head tilted and eyes troubled.

Mud? He leaned down and looked at his face in the side view mirror. The swelling from the fight was all gone thanks to his shifter healing, but the dried blood remained. "That's not mud," he murmured as he wiped his hand over a thick stream that had dried and flaked. "It's blood."

The acrid scent of fear was immediate, and he jerked his attention to the woods to look for the danger that had scared Riley. He'd kill anything that tried to hurt her. But it wasn't the woods that had caused that bitter scent to waft from her skin. She was staring at *him* with wide, frightened eyes. "Why are you covered in blood?"

"It's mine."

"I don't see any cuts."

Nor would she. All of his cuts had healed during the past hour and half it had taken him to get here.

Riley backed up and clutched her duffle bag tighter in front of her.

"Whoa," Drew drawled, holding his hands out like she was a startled animal. "The cut is in my hairline. I fight for extra cash while I'm waiting on logging season to start. Season runs from October to June, and right now, money is tight for me, so I do some boxing on Saturday nights and earn enough for groceries. I just came from there."

"It looks like you got your ass kicked." The nervousness that still lingered in her voice gutted him.

"You should see the other guy," he joked, trying to ease her tension.

"I don't think I would like that."

Drew dropped his hands to his sides and frowned. "You wouldn't like what?"

"I wouldn't like watching you fight."

Worry pooled in her bright eyes, and he heaved a relieved sigh. At least she didn't think he was a monster anymore. He was, no doubt, but at least she didn't know it.

"Here," she said, pulling a bottled water from the side pocket of her luggage. "Oh, I have a washrag, too,

I think." She rummaged through her bag and came up with a dark gray cloth.

Drew muttered his thanks and doused his face with the cool water, then scrubbed it with his hands so he wouldn't get much on the small towel in Riley's outstretched hand.

"Stop, stop, stop," she said, stilling his hand. "You're getting it on your shirt and making it worse. Here, let me."

Drew froze there under her touch, an unsettling sensation of excitement and dread making his stomach clench. The washcloth was soft against his cheek as she ran gentle strokes across his skin, still tingling from the healed cuts and bruises. With a shaky exhalation of breath, he lifted his gaze to hers. Her eyes had softened as she cleaned him. Riley was tough, that much was as plain as the sky was blue, but she was also a caregiver. Another appealing layer to the girl with the odd hair and the baggy clothes.

Damon was a lucky man.

A sense of loss curdled Drew's stomach. Straightening, he took the cloth from Riley's hand and wiped his face clean with a couple of rough strokes. He couldn't afford to get attached to anything or anyone. Losing Mom had proved his bear couldn't handle any kind of bond beyond the Ashe Crew.

"You're cold," he observed gruffly. Even covered in that hideous jacket, she shivered. The sun was high above the mountains, but it was on the cusp of autumn. Though her jacket was baggy and covered most of her, the material was too light for cold October days in the mountains of Wyoming. "Get in the truck and turn the heater on. I'll have this tire fixed shortly, and then I'll take you to Damon Daye." His throat clogged on that last part, and he had to force Damon's name past his lips. His bear was becoming unruly again.

He handed her the washcloth, but hesitated. He wasn't stupid enough to just hand over his DNA to a stranger. "You aren't IESA, are you?"

"I don't know what that is," she muttered through a frown as she wrung the water from the soiled cloth.

Honest notes rang out with each word, and Drew knew he was good. She wasn't a danger to him. If she meant to run one of those fucked up experiments that government agency, IESA, had tried on the Breck Crew, she wouldn't be wasting all that DNA-lush liquid by wringing it out onto the asphalt.

She climbed into his truck and, a moment later, the engine roared to life. He used her distraction to kick the jack out, lift the truck with one hand, shove the new tire on, and settle it back down again with a song of groaning metal. Mom's truck was falling apart, but he'd rather hack off his toes than trade up. This old beater ride was all he had left of her now. Quick as a whip, he tightened the lug nuts back into place and tossed the old tire and tools into the back.

In the truck behind the wheel, he shut the door closed beside him and snuck another glance at Riley. She was hunched forward, hugging the duffle bag to her body, as usual, and her chopped-up hair fell forward to cover her face. Pity. He'd been hoping to get another glance at those clear, wide eyes of hers. It wasn't just the color that had him under a spell, either. Every emotion showed through them. Happiness, fear, humor, reserve. Riley was animated in a way he'd never seen another person be. He wanted to make her laugh just to see her eyes dance and to distract him from the gnawing anger inside of himself. He was ugly on the inside but Riley—soft, human Riley—made him forget that when she smiled.

And now, he was taking her to Damon.

Drew swallowed the snarl in his throat and jerked the truck into drive. Easing back onto the road, he cursed himself for letting his interest in the woman get this far.

She wasn't his, would never be his.

Riley Miller was nothing more than a small detour on his road to destruction.

FOUR

If Drew knew she was pregnant, he didn't show any signs of it. Granted, she was hiding her swollen belly as best she could with the trench coat and her duffle bag. She felt like a liar, but on the off-chance that Seamus tracked her bus route to Saratoga, and if Drew recalled a dark-haired hitchhiker heavy with child, her ex would find her for sure. That man wasn't the type to give up on a hunt, no matter how long it took.

And it wasn't just her safety she had to worry about now. She had a little one to protect until she got the baby to air. Plus, she didn't want Seamus anywhere around Diem and Bruiser Keller, or Damon Daye. They'd been so nice to her already and didn't deserve the trouble that followed her ex around like a shadow.

Drew pulled off the main road and onto a one-lane street paved with pot-holes and gravel.

"Is this Mr. Daye's street?" She fidgeted, growing worried that A—Drew didn't know where he was going or B—he was some kind of ax murderer. He did have the weapon of choice in the back of his truck, just like he'd said earlier.

"Well, he has a highfalutin road that winds around forever if you want to take the scenic route. This is a straight shot to his place, though. It'll probably save us thirty minutes.

"I have a gun," she warned.

Drew took his eyes off the uneven road passing beneath the tires long enough to give her an utterly baffled glare. "What on earth are you running from that has you carrying a gun?"

"I carry it because it's not exactly safe to be hitchhiking around in the mountains. I've seen those cabin horror films. I'm not up for being boiled, skinned, eaten, and then my bones strung up from some tree by my guts while some backwoods creepers chant to the full moon."

"Oh, my God. That was the judgiest thing I've ever heard another person say in my life."

Riley scooted forward and squinted at an approaching sign. *Asheland Mobile Park.* "Are you taking me to a trailer park?"

"*Through* a trailer park and you know what we eat there? Burgers and beer, and sometimes steak if it's payday. Not humans."

The way he said *humans*, as if it were a curse, sent a chill up the back of her neck. She swatted at the skin there and scooted closer to the window. "Are you the only one who lives here?" she asked, scanning the row of old trailers that lined both sides of the street. The community seemed to be completely abandoned.

"No, my crew is up on the landing readying machinery. I told you, logging season starts in a few days."

"Is Damon Daye one of the lumberjacks you work with?"

Drew's single "Ha!" was loud and jarring in such a small space. "No, I can't even imagine Damon

39

cutting and hauling lumber. He owns these mountains. I work for him, and so does the rest of the Ashe Crew."

"Oh. Is that another name for lumberjacks?"

"No, it's the name of the group of people who lives in this trailer park. A couple of other crews work for Damon, too. The Boarlanders cut the trees, and then my crew and the Gray Backs strip the lumber and haul it to the mill in Saratoga." He leaned nearer to her and pointed out the right-hand side. "That's home sweet home. Contain your jealousy."

She giggled before she could stop herself and swatted his finger away from in front of her face. "I bet it fixes up real nice during the holidays."

"You'd be surprised," he murmured as he turned his attention toward the road again.

Riley took a second look at Drew's house. She'd never been in a real trailer park before and had always wondered what the little modular homes were like on the inside. Her apartment wasn't much bigger than the square footage he was likely dealing with, but her home was shaped like a square, while Drew's was long and rectangular. How did living spaces work in a shape like that?

"What do you do for fun out here?" she wondered aloud. "I mean, the closest bar is what, a couple of hours away in Saratoga?"

"I go there on the weekends to watch some of my friends play at Sammy's, but yeah, it's a long drive. Living way out here, you have to get creative with ways to keep yourself entertained."

"So you drink a lot of beer."

Drew snorted and nodded. "Right you are. Beer and hard liquor when the nights get extra long. It's not lonely up here, though. Not like you're probably thinking."

"How do you know what I'm thinking?"

"Woman, every emotion you have is written all over your face."

Troubled, she frowned and turned back to the window, hiding her face from him. "No, it's not."

"It is so, and that ain't a bad thing. I bet you're too honest for your own good."

"If my face gives me away, I'd have to be, right?"

"What about you?" he asked, trapping her momentarily with those icy blue eyes of his. "What do you do for fun in the city?"

"Probably not what you'd think."

41

"Try me. Or do you want me to guess? You hop on and off a subway to meet friends at ritzy bars where the drinks are ten bucks a pop for a watered-down version of a panty-dropper that'll take ten of them to get you a buzz. You ice skate in man-made rinks and walk your dog through perfectly manicured parks where the grass is all sod and no weeds dare to grow. And when your pup poops, you pick it up with some of those plastic dog-shit gloves and smile at the other passersby doing the same thing. You go on company hikes and look down at all the ant-sized people from your high-rise apartment."

"Who's judgy now?"

"Who is joking now? I can't see you as the high-rise type, and you smell like cats, not dogs."

"I smell?" She sniffed her shoulder but didn't smell anything off-putting. Just her natural scent mixed with a hint of deodorant, berry shampoo, and the vanilla body wash she was currently obsessed with.

"You smell like a fucking delicious fruit-tree farm, but underneath it all is a little furry pussy."

Riley narrowed her eyes at him. Drew was a crap-stirrer, just trying to get a rise out of her by using shocking words. "If you must know, I smell like cats because I volunteer for a no-kill, cat-only shelter in my spare time instead of looking down from my second story, modest apartment where people don't look like ants, but like normal-sized people. And I like to re-upholster furniture. I rehab old pieces I find at flea markets and sell them online. That's how I made my living before...well...before."

"Hmm," he said with a slow smile that said he was enjoying peeling away her layers.

This, however, was a dangerous game she couldn't afford to get caught up in. The more Drew found out about her, the more she feared Seamus would somehow find her. All it took was for Drew to say something to these other trailer park Ashe people, who could then talk about her in town and throw down big freaking come-find-me bread crumbs for Seamus to follow.

Riley leaned forward and turned the radio knob until an old country song blared through the staticky speakers.

Drew tossed a questioning glance her way, but didn't push her anymore. Instead, he drove in silence up a winding mountain road and through what looked like a logger worksite with people busily working on machinery and cutting thick cords of metal. Drew waved to a tall, stoic man with eyes so blue, it almost hurt to look at him.

"That's Tagan," Drew said. "He's my boss. He probably passed right by you when you were hitchhiking earlier."

"I thought Damon was your boss," she called over the blaring music.

"Damon's the big boss. Tagan runs this crew."

Drew didn't slow down, but instead took a switchback that led to another gravel road. A few more miles, and he stopped in front of the strangest looking house she'd ever laid eyes on. It was several stories high, if the walls of windows were anything to go by, but it seemed to be built into the side of the mountain. A black Mercedes sat idle in a circle drive, and Drew pulled up right beside the car onto the perfectly manicured lawn.

"I don't think this is a parking space," she muttered.

"And yet I don't feel guilty," Drew said mysteriously. A flash of anger took his eyes before he cooled his expression and replaced it with a mask of indifference. "Now, every time you look out those windows and see my tire tracks, you can think of me."

"Ah, so this is where we part ways. Is this Damon's house?"

"Yep. I'm sure you'll be very comfortable here. He'll take good care of you." The last part was edged with something dark she didn't understand. Bitterness?

"Okay." Riley hesitated, leaning closer to Drew to look up at the mansion out his window. Damon Daye didn't expect her for another week, and suddenly, her nerves kicked in. What if he was angry or wasn't even home? She imagined sleeping the night away curled up on his vast, yet cold-looking front porch. Easing back slightly, she stuck out her hand for a shake. "I guess I'll probably never see you again, so...goodbye Drew Hudson."

A strand of blond hair fell forward into his face, and she resisted the urge to touch it. His eyes seemed to have lightened, but perhaps it was a trick of the saturated afternoon light that reflected off the hood of his truck. His gaze dipped to her lips, and her heart stuttered in her chest. Breath frozen in her lungs, she stilled under his hungry gaze.

He brushed his fingertips across her cheek, and then slowly he cupped the back of her neck. Leaning forward, he smiled just before he pressed his lips to hers. Her eyes rolled closed as she leaned into his touch. His lips softened, moved with hers, plucked at her lips until his tongue brushed the sensitive flesh just inside her mouth. And when she melted against him, his reaction was nothing as she had hoped.

Drew pulled back.

Searching her eyes, he brushed the pad of his thumb over her cheekbone once more. Riley hadn't had a single drink since she'd signed the surrogate contract, but she remembered this feeling. This was two quick shots of cheap tequila. And now her blood was heating to boiling and her panties were slowly soaking. She hadn't touched herself in months, but suddenly, her body was aching to be closer to Drew. To be caressed by him. A few gentle touches, and Drew made her feel adored in a way Seamus hadn't managed in all the time they'd been together.

"Thanks for today," he said in a low, gravelly voice. "It's been a while since I smiled. It felt good."

Riley couldn't find any words that fit her stumbling thoughts, so she simply said, "You're welcome."

"Have a nice life, Riley Miller."

Oh, this really was the goodbye now. Okay. "Yep," she said lamely. Scrunching up her nose, she pushed open the door and slid out, covering her belly with the duffle bag still. "You too. Have a nice life." She cleared her throat as he pulled her door closed from the inside. "In the trailer park, I mean. And good luck with, you know, lumberjacking."

God, she was so mixed up. Hormones raging as she took in his sad smile, she gave an awkward wave and marched toward the door, determined not to look back and make more of an ass of herself.

As the sound of his roaring engine began to fade, she turned and took one last peek at the man who'd gotten her here safely and made her forget about her problems for a little while. He'd thanked her for making him smile. She should've thanked him back since he'd done the same for her.

All she knew was that with a belly swollen with child and a mountain of trouble back home, she'd stumbled across a man who stirred up emotions she'd never felt before.

And now, it suddenly seemed tragic that she'd

never see him again.

FIVE

Drew watched Riley grow smaller and smaller from the rearview and winced as the animal inside threatened to shred him. Dammit, he couldn't pull over and Change here. He was too close to her. Bear would charge right back there and scare the piss out of her.

Drew gritted his teeth, fighting for control. She was in Damon's care now. He'd show her Castle Daye and provide her with whatever she needed. She'd never want for anything. Sure, Damon was cold and was only just now coming around to opening up again after several centuries of hardening his heart, but he had money and connections. He owned businesses and had a future that stretched on for eternity.

And where was Drew going? To hell, and fast. The Ashe Crew wasn't out in the public—not yet— and Riley was utterly human. She was basically organs wrapped in rice paper. These woods and this uncertain life were no place for a woman like her. Now Brooke, Skyler, Danielle, Everly, and Diem? They were all bear and falcon shifters except for Danielle, and even she was a nature nerd adept at keeping herself alive in rough terrain. Women could make it just the same as men out here, but for as tough as she talked, Riley was a wounded bird. It was the moments in between her popping off with her bravado that he'd seen the vulnerability and fear in her eyes. Drew shook his head and muttered a curse.

The women of the Ashe Crew belonged to these woods, just as surely as the lumberjacks they'd mated to. Riley, however, belonged tucked away in Damon's castle. Safe from the danger that surrounded bear-shifter life and safe from the monster in his middle that would surely ruin her if given half the chance.

Maybe if he'd met her before Mom had died...

Loss bowed him forward over the steering wheel. He would've stood a chance at making a woman like Riley happy before, but now he was a shell with no substance.

What could he offer her?

Not a damned thing of importance.

By the time he pulled up to the landing where he and the others would be working the lumber in a few days' time, his mood had plummeted. Back to reality where his bear was a holy terror clawing at his insides and where Tagan had just banned him from the thing that kept him steady—bare-knuckle, no-rules boxing. Friggin' A.

"Who was that in your truck?" Tagan asked the second he slid out from behind the wheel.

"None of your fuckin' business." Every word was a snarl, but Tagan was crossing into dangerous territory right now. Drew was already pissed, and the alpha knew better than to press his members when they were riled up like this. Did he not smell the damned bear in him? Even to his own nose, Drew reeked of fur and anger. "I'm going to help Bruiser set up the skyline."

"Drew," Tagan snapped, his voice crackling with

power.

Drew turned slowly, allowing a snarl to curl his lip. "More orders, *alpha*?"

Tagan's face went burgundy. "Stand down, Drew."

Drew swallowed hard and grunted against the weight that pressed him toward the dirt beneath him. His knees buckled.

"It's been two months, and you've chosen not to deal with what's happened. At the risk of my crew." Tagan angled his chin and glared him down, his eyes lightening to a snowy color. "Get your shit together, Hudson."

Drew fell to his knees.

"Tagan!" his mate, Brooke, yelled. "Stop it."

A long, feral growl rippled through Tagan's throat, but one look at his mate, and his lips fell back over his teeth. She was a buck twenty of pissed-off blonde, their toddler Wyatt clinging to her hip.

"Can you not see he's hurting?"

"It's been two months—"

"Two months nothing, Tagan," she gritted out as she approached. "We don't all deal at the same pace."

"He hasn't dealt at all!"

"No, no, no," Wyatt said, scrunching up his little nose and shaking his chubby little finger at his alpha father. Right now, that was one of three words in the kid's entire vocabulary. Denison had taught him how to say *pecker* and, naturally, he knew *momma*.

Drew would've snickered if this was at all funny. Unfortunately, he was stuck in the mud with his neck exposed while his alpha had a spat with his lady.

"You think cowing him is going to help him?" Brooke asked, arching one delicate golden brow.

Drew cleared his throat. "Can I get up?"

Tagan didn't say anything, just threw him a dangerous look and marched off. The farther away he got, the less weight pressed against Drew's shoulders until he was finally able to stand.

"I'm sorry," Brooke said low. "Tagan's had a lot on his plate trying to figure out what to do about coming out to the public. The decision is torturing him, and you aren't making things any easier. Drew, you've been a loose cannon for two months. Now, you know I love you. We all do, and we're worried about you. You'll come to dinner at our trailer tonight, and you and Tagan will work this out."

"I wouldn't be good dinner company tonight—"

"Didn't say it was a request, Drew. Dinner is at eight after you are all done working." Brooke turned and strode for a batch of trees where she'd set up her painting easel.

Wyatt was all wide blue eyes and mussed dark hair when he pointed at Drew and said, "Pecker."

Fantastic.

With a growl, Drew stomped off toward the giant pine Bruiser was stripping to hang the skyline from. He wanted to kick everything.

After pulling work gloves from his back pocket, Drew gathered a pile of newly cut limbs and dragged them away. The last thing they needed was a snake den beneath their skyline. Bruiser was high above, strapped to the tree and dropping limbs every few seconds.

Thank goodness for work. Drew could be mindless here. Hard labor, sweat, and the stretch of long unused muscles settled his animal. Not like Riley had been able to do with those wide eyes of hers and that wry quirk to her full lips, but still, it was something.

And just like that, there she was again, taking up all the space in his head. His dick hardened and throbbed against the seam of his pants, and he tried to think of anything else to ease his boner. Like washing dishes. There. That was the least sexy thing ever. Unless he was washing dishes with Riley, standing behind her while she rinsed the suds off a dinner plate as he pressed against her back and pulled her earlobe between his teeth and *shit*. His pants were even tighter now.

He reached for the bigger limbs and focused on moving as much as possible at once, and after a few minutes, that helped.

Bruiser, donning spike boots, climbed down the skyline pole and nodded a wary greeting. "You gonna bite my head off today?"

Oh, right. Yesterday Drew had been on a tear with anyone who talked to him. Come to think of it, today he hadn't been much better. "I won't unless you're going to push therapy time on me."

"Man, you need some of that. Do you remember Changing last night?"

"What?" Drew dropped the heavy limbs in his arms and stared at Bruiser in horror. "No, I didn't."

Bruiser's dark eyebrows lifted, and he nodded once. "Yeah, you did. You were roaring right outside the trailer park. Woke everyone up. Sleep walking now, are we?"

Or sleep-Changing, and that was terrifying. His bear was not to be trusted right now.

"Hey, is your father-in-law looking for a consort?"

With a baffled look, Bruiser shook his head. "I don't even know what that means. Like a fuck buddy?"

"I guess. I mean, obviously he's lonely, so it's not that surprising he would bring a woman up to his mansion. It's kind of weird that he chose a human, though—"

"Wait, what are you talking about? Damon isn't looking for a mate. What human?"

"The human I just took to his house. She said she was expected."

Bruiser's dark eyes went wide. "Was her name Riley?"

"Yeeesss," Drew drawled out slow.

"Shit, I've got to go. Was Diem at Damon's house?"

"I don't know. Isn't she supposed to be working today?" Drew hesitated, then called out at Bruiser's receding back, "I didn't go inside."

The slamming of Bruiser's door on his truck echoed down the mountain. The engine roared to life a split second later, and then Bruiser peeled out, tossing gravel and mud behind him until his tires caught traction.

Huh. Bruiser knew Riley.

Drew's gaze followed Bruiser's mud-covered pickup as it sped up the washed-out logging road.

What had that little human done to catch the attention of a berserker bear and a death-bringer dragon?

SIX

Riley's sneakers squeaked against the huge, white marble tiles that spanned the grand hallway. If she didn't know better, she'd say this place was a museum, not a house.

A man who'd introduced himself as Mason walked slowly in front of her. Geez, he was huge. He wasn't a tall man, but his shoulders looked as wide as the broad side of a barn. Was everyone around here lifting weights all day and eating loads of protein?

Grand chandeliers lit their way toward a large set of wooden double doors. Mason smiled kindly at her and knocked.

"Come in," came the muffled reply.

Mason pushed the door open and strode into the room, introducing her. "Mr. Daye, this is Riley Miller."

The man behind a sprawling mahogany desk looked up at her with surprise. When he stood, he was tall and lean with a runner's build. His medium gray business suit had been pressed to perfection. His hair was dark as night, but at his temples, the slightest hint of silver was beginning to form. His face, however, made it impossible to guess his age. His smooth skin didn't boast blemishes, or crow's feet, or even smile lines.

"Ms. Miller, I wasn't expecting you for another week. Have you run into trouble?" His eyes widened as he stepped around the desk. "Is the baby all right?"

"Yes, of course." Riley pulled off her coat and angled herself to the side so he could see her very pregnant belly. "She's fine. The doctor says she's healthy as a horse."

Mason snorted behind her, but when she turned, he was standing motionless near the doorway.

"Great." Damon took a deep, steadying breath as he approached. "That's great news. And please, don't apologize. I'm happy you've come now. As you know, if it were my choice, you would've been here the entire pregnancy. I respected your wish to continue with your life until the delivery date approached, though. Was the money I sent you enough? Shall I give you more?"

"No." Riley shook her head and repeated, "No. I've actually got the money you sent right here. I wanted to give it back." She pulled the envelope from her duffle bag and offered it to him. When he crossed his arms over his chest, refusing, she explained. "I know it was drawn up in our contract you would pay me a certain amount, but I didn't want to be a surrogate for money. I did it because I wanted to do something nice. And Diem and Bruiser's letter left its mark on me. I wanted to help them start a family, not get rich. I can make my own way, sir."

"Ms. Miller—"

"Riley, please. You are the grandfather of the child I'm carrying. It kind of makes us family until I deliver."

Damon's stoic face softened, and he nodded. "Riley, I didn't give you the money because I thought you were a charity case. I gave it to you so you could be comfortable while you are growing my granddaughter. You see, she is very important to me, and to my daughter and son-in-law. More important than you could ever imagine, and we're eternally grateful you have chosen our family to help. It's a very selfless thing you are doing, but I'd feel better if you'd let me compensate you for your time and effort."

"You've already paid all my doctor bills, Mr. Daye. And you got me in to see that specialist in record time when my morning sickness got to be overwhelming. I know I'm a week early, but I could use a place to stay until the delivery if you'll have me. That's payment enough."

"Done. You'll have a room made up, a key to the house, access to my driver, any food you desire and crave, and the money. Deal?"

Wait, that didn't feel like a compromise at all. "You're not going to let me give this money back, are you?"

A small smile took his lips as he shook his head.

"Okay, deal."

"Mason, go pull Diem from her office and tell her she has an important visitor." When the large man left to do Damon's bidding, Mr. Daye leaned forward with a mischievous smile. "I want to be here when Diem sees your stomach for the first time. It isn't customary for my people to be overly emotional about anything, but I must confess, I've rather enjoyed watching my daughter prepare to become a mother over this last year."

Riley giggled and nodded. "I've been excited, too, especially to meet you and the Kellers."

Damon retrieved a cold bottled water for her from a miniature fridge behind his desk while Riley straightened her sweater over her stretchy maternity jeans. She'd worn a fitted outfit today so Diem could see the pregnancy better when she met her for the first time. It was an enormous relief to be out of that heavy trench coat.

She sipped water and shuffled her feet, eyes on the door as her nerves kicked in. Sure, she'd talked to Diem on the phone a lot, probably more than any friend she'd ever had, but it was different meeting someone in person. Down the hall, she could hear the clacking of Mason's shoes and the squeaking of someone following.

Riley made an *O* shape with her lips and exhaled slowly. This was it. The counselor had said the first meeting would be awkward, but they would settle into a comfort with each other eventually. For that, she was prepared. She'd imagined this moment a hundred times.

After setting the water bottle down, she clasped her hands behind her back and faced the door.

Her heart was beating against her chest as if it wanted to eject from her body.

Mason entered. *Here we go.*

A dark-haired woman with porcelain white skin and amber colored eyes like her father's entered. She wore comfortable-looking jeans with holes at the knees and sneakers much like Riley's. Her expression was questioning, but when her gaze dipped to Riley's belly, her face crumpled completely.

"Oh, my goodness," Diem said, voice thick. She approached slowly, and Riley prepared for the awkwardness.

Diem jogged the last few feet and wrapped her up tight in a hug. The woman's shoulders shook with quiet sobs, and Riley patted her hesitantly, then wrapped her arms around her and hugged her close. Tears burned her own eyes as she imagined how much of a relief the woman must be feeling.

"Oh!" Diem gasped, easing back and staring at Riley's stomach.

"Yeah," Riley said with an emotional laugh. "She gets feisty if you crowd her space." When the baby bumped her again, she grabbed Diem's hand and pressed it over the spot the baby was kicking or elbowing.

Diem's dark eyes were rimmed with tears as she knelt down in front of Riley. "Hi, Harper."

The baby rolled languidly, moving Riley's entire stomach. "Harper. I think she likes it. That's a beautiful name."

"Thank you," Diem whispered, as if she didn't want to break the magic of the moment. "Bruiser came up with it."

A shadow darkened the doorway, and Riley looked up to see a muscled behemoth standing splay-legged in the doorway, breathing heavy. His hair was short and dark, and his eyes a strange green-gold color. Chest heaving, he strode slowly into the room and offered his hand for a shake. His manner was much more reserved than his wife's. Riley shook it and introduced herself.

"Horace Keller," he said in a gravelly voice.

"Friends call me Bruiser. You're early. I wanted to be at the airport when you landed to pick you up."

"I took the bus. Sorry for not giving notice. It was a last minute decision to come up here right now instead of waiting."

"I'm glad you came," he murmured, eyes still on her undulating belly and one hand stroking Diem's hair.

His wife stood and asked, "May I?" She held Bruiser's hand palm out.

Bruiser ducked his chin, looking decidedly uncomfortable. "No, it's okay."

Riley smiled her understanding and said, "I don't mind at all. I'm not uncomfortable with touch, and she's your daughter after all."

"My daughter." The soft words left Bruiser's lips like a prayer.

Tears streaked down Diem's cheeks as she pressed her husband's hand against where Harper was moving the most. A soft gasp left his lips, and he looked up at Riley, a startled expression on his face. She laughed and nodded. "Welcome to my world. Harper has been active since sixteen weeks. Especially at night when I'm trying to sleep. You're going to have a little party animal on your hands when she gets here."

"Can we tell everyone now?" Bruiser asked Diem, a hopeful smile splitting his face.

"I think we should."

"I don't know why you waited," Damon murmured from behind them where he leaned against his desk with his arms crossed and a lingering smile on his face.

"Well, because we just wanted to make sure the baby was okay before we got all of their hopes up."

"Tell who?" Riley asked curiously.

"The Ashe Crew."

Riley froze. "The Ashe Crew of lumberjacks?"

"How did you know?" Diem asked.

"Because I kissed Drew." Heat blasted into Riley's cheeks at the slip-up. "*Met* Drew. I meant to say I met Drew…Hudson. The lumberjack who is also part of the Ashe Crew." She scrunched up her face as the Kellers stared at her. Clearing her throat, she nodded once. "Yep." There was that awkwardness the counselor had warned her about.

Bruiser narrowed his eyes at her in an unsettlingly thoughtful expression, but it was Diem who saved her from the scrutiny. "I'm going to get her settled into a room," she announced, tugging Riley's hand and leading her toward the door.

The room she led her to was actually an elevator ride away, and then down another long marble hallway lined with half-naked statues of Grecian-style men and women. As beautiful as this house was, Riley found herself afraid to touch anything for fear of smudging her fingerprints on something.

"Okay," Diem murmured, closing a thick, refurbished wooden door behind her. "Lay it on me. What's going on?"

"What? Nothing," Riley lied.

"Then why does your hair look all chopped up like you did it yourself in some cheap motel, and why is half your duffle bag full of socks?"

Hmm, Diem was extremely observant. Riley tried and failed to zip up her too-full luggage and tossed it onto a king-size bed with a towering headboard suited for royalty. She lay on the bed and spread her arms and legs like a star. She frowned up at the mural of muscular men wearing next to nothing. Their penises must be extravagantly small to fit behind those tiny fig leaves.

"My ex is a bit of a jerk about the whole surrogacy thing. It was just easier for me to come out here now instead of next week. The reason my bag is half full of socks is because I packed in a hurry and wasn't thinking clearly."

"Riley," Diem said in a careful tone, sinking down onto the bed beside her. "I'm going to tell you this one time, and then I'll let it rest. You're safe here, but it's best if we know if there is something we need to keep you safe from."

Unable to admit her fears about Seamus out loud, Riley nodded. "If I think I'm in trouble, I'll tell you first."

"Okay. Now, your hair. You're free to leave it like that, but I can even it up a bit if you like."

Riley sat straight up. "Really?" If she and Drew crossed paths again, she wanted him to see more than a street urchin.

"Yes, really."

"Diem, can I ask you another favor?"

"Anything." She leveled her with such an honest look that relief slid the weight off Riley's shoulders.

"When you go tell the Ashe Crew about Harper, would you mind if I go with you?"

A knowing smile spread across Diem's face, but she didn't mention Drew or tease her, which made Riley like the woman even more. "Of course. I think it's only right you come. It'll get you out of this stuffy house, too." Diem stood and sauntered off toward an open on-suite bathroom. "I'd bring your duffle bag if I were you when we go."

"Why? I thought I was staying here?"

Diem cast her a beaming grin before she said, "Asheland Mobile Park might not look like much, but magic happens there."

Riley followed behind slowly. She couldn't imagine wanting to stay in a dingy, dirty old trailer park over this place, but she'd only just met Diem and didn't want to argue. Instead, Riley would bring her duffle bag to appease the woman.

Magic didn't exist in her world.

Just the dark reality of fear and broken promises, and the singular goal to get this baby safely delivered to make up for some of the harm she'd done.

SEVEN

Riley smoothed her hair with her hand again in an attempt to stifle the nerves fluttering around in her belly. Harper was definitely asleep, so this was all jitters caused by the fact she could very well see Drew again.

Her hair was really short now, stacked in the back and longer up front in what Diem called an asymmetrical cut. Whatever the name, Riley was utterly impressed with Diem's creativity with scissors. This haircut was as good as any she'd gotten in the cheap salon in the shopping center near her apartment—perhaps better.

Bruiser was humming along to a country song on the radio with his elbow resting on the open window. Diem had a dreamy smile on her lips from her seat in between her and Bruiser, and she kept glancing at Riley's belly. Every time she did, Riley warmed from the inside out. She was doing the right thing.

With a sigh, Riley caught the air currents outside the window with her open palm. Even though the night was cold, she felt all warm and glowing in her figure hugging sweater, skinny maternity jeans and lace-up snow boots she'd packed just in case it was as cold as the Internet had said when she researched Wyoming. No more hiding her silhouette now. For the first time since she'd left Minneapolis, she felt like she could loosen up and forget about her troubles for a while.

And she was going to see Drew again.

Illuminating the woods, twinkling lights flashed near and far. "Look!" she said breathlessly as she pointed to the trees.

"The fireflies come out when it's cool," Bruiser said, a smile in his voice.

"They're beautiful out here." Perhaps Diem had been right about magic after all. Stunned, Riley leaned forward and rested her chin against her folded arms as Bruiser guided the truck down a steep switchback.

"About Drew," Diem said in a soft voice. "He's not in the best place right now."

"What do you mean? What's the matter with him?" Riley asked, swinging around to her.

Diem and Bruiser gave each other a loaded look.

"He's lost someone close to him, and his inner...well, he's hurting. I just wanted to warn to you be careful with him. For both of you."

"Okay, noted." Disappointment pierced her chest cavity as Riley looked out at the lit trailer park ahead. Drew was more complicated than some smart-talking, stranger-kissing, Adonis. It made sense now. Even though his mouth had been bracketed by sexy smile lines, she'd had to drag out every teeny ghost of a grin from him.

She understood loss. She'd buried family and friends before, but that wasn't what had caused her to hunch into herself, shielding her heart from the world. She'd lost herself two years ago and had fought and clawed to transform into someone new. Someone who was less broken than she used to be, but she'd never replace the person she was. The old Riley and all of the parts she loved about herself were dead. Never in her life would she wish the pain of loss on anyone. Especially Drew, who'd shown her kindness and made her heart thump back to life with that unexpected kiss of his.

She was here until Harper was delivered, and then she would head home to sort out the mess with Seamus. Was she stupid to face-off with her dangerous ex? She liked to think not. It wasn't stupidity that would push her to reclaim her life in her hometown. She wasn't a runner. The only reason she'd left recently was because of the baby. She didn't want to endanger Harper's life in the battle. But someday, someway, she was going to make Seamus let her get on with the life she'd fought to create in Minneapolis.

Diem was right. Throwing interest at Drew would only bring trouble to them both.

A raucous group sat in colorful plastic chairs around a giant bonfire when Bruiser pulled the truck through the back entrance to the park. One of them, a fine-boned woman with dark hair and bright green eyes stood telling a story to the laughter of the group.

Riley couldn't take her eyes off the woman. She radiated confidence—held her own in front of all those burly men. She held their attention rapt, and when she looked up and caught Riley staring, she offered a friendly wave.

Riley lifted two fingers and smiled. The truck screeched to a stop in front of a trailer with a red door. Everywhere, outdoor lights were strung from house to house and hung from poles along the gravel street, immersing the entire park in a warm glow. Riley opened the door, slid from the truck, and waited for Diem to slip out next.

"This is Tagan and Brooke's house. They are like king and queen of this trailer park." Bruiser rested his hands on both of their lower backs and guided them up the creaking, splintered steps. "Don't be nervous, though," he said as an aside to Riley. "Tagan is one of my oldest friends and the best dude I know."

Bruiser stepped forward and knocked. Moths and gnats buzzed around the single porch light, and behind them, a purple bug light zapped. One bug down, a billion to go.

"Come in," a woman called from inside.

Bruiser opened the door and stood aside for

Riley and Diem to enter. They were met by the most adorable toddler clad in a diaper and the remains of what looked like a spaghetti dinner.

"Sorry," a blond-haired woman apologized. "We're just finishing up dinner, and this little one is fast! Hi, I'm Brooke." The petite woman held out her hand for a shake, and Riley clasped it quickly and released, grateful Brooke was nice and welcoming, even while chasing a rambunctious, giggling baby.

"Riley Miller. Your son is adorable," she said with a smile, ignoring the pang of sadness that always washed through her when she saw a baby. Her pregnancy was for Diem and Bruiser, she reminded herself, biting her lip as punishment for her lack of control over her maternal instincts.

When she looked up at the two men who stood near a small kitchen table, she froze. One man, Tagan likely, stared at her with a troubled look through his blinding blue eyes, while Drew stared openly at her stomach.

"What the hell?" Drew said on a breath. "Are you pregnant?"

Riley laughed nervously. "Obviously."

"No, not fucking obviously. I kissed a pregnant

75

woman."

"Uck, uck," the toddler chanted.

An odd, wild sound emanated from Drew as he stepped around the table. "Can I talk to you? Alone?"

Why did she feel like she was taking a long walk to the principal's office when she followed him outside?

"Is it Damon's?" he asked, turning on her, eyes a feral, searing blue.

"What?"

"The baby. Whose is it?"

She reared back, feeling utterly slapped. "Not that it's any of your business, but it's Bruiser's."

"The fuck?" His voice wrenched up an octave. "No, no, no, that's not how it works. Bruiser's mated and bonded. He's Diem's, and she's his."

"Mated? Drew, I don't understand, and why are you mad? This doesn't have anything to do with you."

"It does!" He hooked his hands on his hips and glared at the bonfire. With a sigh, he dragged his attention back to her and lowered his voice. "It feels like it does. So…you're Bruiser's? Or Damon's?"

"Drew," Riley cradled her stomach in her hands and shook her head. "I'm not anyone's. I only just met

Damon today, right after you dropped me off. I'm here for Bruiser and Diem."

Tagan let off an ear-splitting whistle from his front porch behind her and waved to those gathered around the bonfire. Bruiser gestured her up onto the porch with him and Diem, and Riley shot Drew one last confused frown before she stepped up beside them. He looked ill.

When the small crowd had settled in front of them, Bruiser cast them an emotional smile. "We have something we want to tell you all. Something we probably should've told you earlier, but with this stuff, everything is uncertain until the end. But…" He looked at Diem as she clasped Riley's hand and squeezed it. "Diem and I are going to have a baby girl. Harper Keller will be joining us via this wonderful, selfless woman in a couple of weeks. We signed our contracts with her last year, and she's been taking care of our Harper."

The murmur of the crowd transitioned to a deafening volume as everyone charged the tiny porch. Bruiser was laughing as he tried to talk. "Careful with her. She's carrying precious cargo." His body shook as a tall man with blond hair clapped him on the back.

The same man turned to her and bowed. "My respect to the Vessel of the Dragon."

"Kellen!" the dark-haired woman who'd been telling the story beside the fire exclaimed. "She's human."

"Skyler!" Brooke said with a hard shake of her head.

Riley stood frozen. She didn't understand the dynamics here. She didn't understand why they were calling her a human, or why the strange-talking man had called her "Vessel of the Dragon." She shrank away from them until her hips bumped the porch railing.

"Give her space," Drew gritted out.

"Why?" A man with chestnut, close-cropped hair rasped out, as if he had no voice at all. An angry red scar glistened against his neck.

"Brighton," Drew said. "I swear to God I'll rip your fucking face off if you don't give her space.

"Is she yours?" Kellen asked. "Vessel of the Dragon and Mate of the Beast."

"Kellen," Tagan muttered, holding his hands out toward Drew in a calming gesture. "Kindly shut the fuck up. Drew, look at me. Look at me!"

A low snarl filled the air, and Riley stifled a scream when Drew lifted inhuman ice-colored eyes to Tagan.

"We're backing off. Brighton, move away from her. Bruiser, you, too."

Bruiser had placed himself in front of Riley and was now crouching slightly as the same feral sound rattled his throat. "I can't," he growled out.

"It's not a request, Bruiser," Tagan said calmly. "It's an order. Let Drew get to her."

"I. Can't. That's my baby in her."

Drew shook his head slowly, and an empty smile curled up his lip. "No. Mine." His voice was deep and gravelly—unrecognizable from the man Riley had talked to earlier.

Tagan said, "Drew. Bear. The baby is Bruiser's."

"My mate. My cub."

Bruiser leapt across the porch just as Drew's frame vibrated and shattered. An enormous grizzly bear blasted out of Drew, roaring so loud it rattled the ground beneath Riley's feet. Bruiser wasn't Bruiser anymore. He was fur and claws and glowing gold-green eyes as he clamped impossibly long canines into Drew-the-fucking-monster's shoulder.

Riley screamed as the brawling animals smashed in the the porch, ripping the wooden decking from the trailer and making her lose her balance.

A strong hand clamped onto her arm and yanked her inside Tagan's house. Brighton, Drew had called him.

A few others ran in behind them before he slammed the door closed.

"I don't understand," Riley whispered in horror and denial, but everything was clicking quietly into place. Tagan just addressed Drew as *Bear*. Kellen had called her *human*. She'd watched the news with the rest of the world when bear shifters had come out to the public in Breckenridge. Oh, she was beginning to see just what camp of people she'd found herself immersed in. The Ashe Crew were bear shifters.

"I think you do," Brighton rasped out, his voice barely a whisper. He winced as if the words had hurt to push out of his throat.

Riley looked from him to the door where the roaring of the bears filled her head. When Harper squirmed, she cradled her belly, then dragged her gaze to Diem. "He called Harper his cub."

"I'm so sorry," Diem said thickly. "I wanted to tell you, to be up front in the contract, but we were advised by our lawyer not to. We haven't come out to the public. And then I met you, and you were so nice, and you've been through so much—"

"What does that mean?" she snapped, wiping the back of her hand against her damp cheeks and standing rigid.

"I mean I know. Bruiser and my father and I know."

"You know? You know!" Riley looked around at the questioning faces around her in disbelief, then out at the brawl she could see through the bent blinds in the front picture window. There were more bears fighting now. Bears! "Why did you choose me to be your surrogate then? There had to be a billion better candidates out there."

"Because," Diem said around a sob, "It was my choice. I saw your profile, saw how hard you'd worked to become one, and you felt right. I've had it hard, too." Her voice softened, and she looked around the room. "We all have. It didn't feel right to choose someone who was perfect on paper. I wanted someone with fight in them. And besides that, I knew

what you were after."

"Yeah? And what's that?"

"Redemption."

Riley shook her head slowly, unable to hold anyone's gaze anymore. "So you think you know everything, and yet I know nothing about any of you. Is Harper a bear to?"

"Riley," Diem said, warning in her tone. "Ask that question in a few days when you've gotten to know us first."

"Is she a bear?" Riley yelled.

Diem's delicate nostrils flared slightly as she inhaled a deep breath. "She might be a bear, and she might be something else."

Riley arched her eyebrows, waiting.

Diem lifted her chin. "If we're lucky, she'll be a dragon, like me."

EIGHT

Riley guffawed at what Diem had just said. "A dragon. A dragon? Like a flying, fire-breathing, treasure-hoarding dragon?" She put her hands protectively in front of her belly and backed up until her back hit a wall.

"Probably not a fire-breather," Brighton rasped out. "Diem doesn't have the fire like Damon does."

"Oh," she said, nodding hysterically in a very bobble-head like fashion. "That's great. Damon's a dragon, too. I'm surrounded by bears and friggin' dragons. Anything else?"

Skyler lifted her hand hesitantly, like a child in

kindergarten. "Falcon."

A screech of utter frustration and disbelief scratched up Riley's throat. "I think I need some time alone."

Brooke, who'd been silently watching from the kitchen table until now, stood. "The fight sounds like it's over. I'll take you to ten-ten."

"Okay." Why was she still nodding like a lunatic? "Is that some sort of dungeon?"

Brooke's eyes were so sad. "No. It's a trailer like this one. It's also where most of the women here started to get to know this place."

Sounded like a dungeon to her.

Cradling her belly, Riley followed Brooke outside. She searched for the bears who'd been fighting a minute ago, but all she could see were large, lumbering shadowy figures headed for the woods beside the trailer park.

Brooke's little boy was asleep in the woman's arms, sucking his thumb.

"Will Harper hurt me?" Riley blurted out suddenly.

"No. She won't have her first shift until she is at least a year old. You'll deliver a little baby girl who looks and smells and acts just like every other baby girl. You know," she said, waiting for Riley to catch up. "I used to be human, too. And when I found out bear shifters existed, I was upset. I was shocked and angry at being Turned, and I felt all of those confusing emotions you're going through right now."

Brooke led her across the street and up a set of dilapidated stairs to a cream-colored trailer with green shutters. It was ancient looking, and the paint was peeling around the door frame. Even the number *1010* was hanging sideways by a lone, rusty nail.

Brooke walked straight through a tiny living room to a narrow hallway to a bedroom. Paintings of a man's face were scattered in one of the corners.

"I know it doesn't look like much, but I wanted to show you where I started healing from an attack by a mugger that left me shaken to my core. These paintings are mine, and this used to be a studio for me. I don't know what you've been through, but it's something big from the way Diem was talking. You don't have to tell anyone about it unless you want to, and we won't push you, but know this." Brooke turned to Riley with wide, serious eyes. "Here, you're safe."

"But Drew and Bruiser—"

"Were being bullheaded men, but they'd never hurt you. I think Drew is having a problem with his bear. He's grown protective of you in a way I've never seen him be toward anyone. He shouldn't have challenged Bruiser like that, and you shouldn't have found out what he is like this, but be patient with him. He's a little lost right now."

"He called me his mate," Riley whispered. A trill of hope and confusion surged through her just saying that. Even at his scariest, he hadn't been focused on her. He'd been focused on protecting her from Brighton getting too close when she'd panicked.

"Yeah," Brooke murmured. "There's that. Which is why he is probably getting protective of that baby you're carrying. You just came in here and shook everything up, didn't you?" Brooke winked and bumped her shoulder against Riley's, then walked out of the room. "There's clean sheets on the bed and towels in the cabinet in the bathroom."

"Thank you," Riley said on a breath, swaying under the weight of all the new information.

It was a lot. Too much for one person to shoulder at once, perhaps. She'd known bear shifters existed, but it was a completely different thing to watch the man she was crushing on turn into a damned giant grizzly.

First Seamus, the monster, and then Drew, a different kind of monster. She was a wreck with men.

Arms and legs feeling like lead, she shuffled numbly across the living room, through the tiny eat-in kitchen with its white-washed cabinets, faux-wood countertops, and a giant dead spider near the sink, then into the master bedroom.

The space was much larger than she'd anticipated. Cheap laminate wood flooring ran the length of the room under a queen-size bed with two antique sconces on either side of the headboard. She tried to imagine Brooke as anything but the strong woman she seemed to be now, but failed. She just couldn't fathom her in this place, painting those pictures of that man with the cruel twist to his lips— her attacker.

Desperate for something familiar, she pulled a pair of fluffy towels from the stark white cabinet above an old washer and dryer in the bathroom. She undressed slowly as the tap water transitioned from frigid to boiling hot. Inside the old swamp mud-colored bathtub, she hunched forward under the hot jets of water and locked her elbows against the cheap plastic side of the shower. Disguised as tiny drops of moisture streaming down her cheeks, fear and anger left her body.

She should've been told she was carrying a shifter. She couldn't think of Harper as a dragon or a bear yet, but Diem should've made the choice up to her whether she carried a shifter child or not. Their existence wasn't this huge secret like it used to be. The Breck Crew were the faces of the shifter movement. They'd been accepted and, in some ways, celebrated over the last eighteen months since they'd come out to the public.

But what if Diem had told her? Would it have mattered after a few days of letting it sink in? It didn't really change the letter she'd read from Diem and Bruiser that had outlined their struggle to have a child. Diem couldn't carry for medical reasons.

It wouldn't have changed her reasons for choosing to do this either. She'd applied to agencies that matched surrogates with parents, but she hadn't fit the requirements. She hadn't given birth before and was unproven as a viable womb. She was single and coming off a public traumatic event that had been highly publicized and would be on file with any agency. She'd hired her own lawyer, who searched for couples who were willing to deal with the uncertainty of Riley's life. Diem and Bruiser had been the only ones to answer. If she'd known they were shifters, trying for a child that would someday be like them, would it really have mattered?

Perhaps it would have for a few days or a week, but Riley was pro-shifter. She'd even voted they shouldn't have to register publicly like the government wanted them to. The vote had swung the other way, and they were supposed to register, but not many of them had. The Ashe Crew definitely hadn't.

But how much did that change how she felt about the little baby doing summersaults in her stomach? Riley looked down at her belly and sighed. Not a damned bit.

"I'm sorry," Drew said in a muffled voice from the other side of the shower curtain.

Riley jumped and covered herself with a teeny washrag. It didn't hide much.

She stuck her head around the curtain, careful to

keep the ends tucked to cover her soppy wet and naked body. "What are you doing in here?" Her voice was shrill, but one look at Drew had her swallowing a string of curses down.

He sat on the closed lid of the toilet, head in his hands, every muscle tensed as if he were in pain. A giant claw mark ran the length of his ribcage and tapered off just above the jeans that clung to his hips. When he looked up at her, his eyes weren't that wild color anymore. They were a soft blue and filled with regret.

Riley eased back into the shower so she didn't have to see the pain on his face. "You were out of control out there," she murmured, squirting an entire miniature bottle of shampoo into her hand.

"I know."

"My last boyfriend was an overprotective, jealous asshole who stifled me. I don't want that again."

"Nor do you deserve that."

Closing her eyes, she scrubbed the fruity smelling wash into her short tresses. "Well, make your apologies then."

"The person I am today isn't the man I want to

be. That overprotective asshole you saw out there isn't me. Not normally. And I bet your ex told you that, too, because that's what men like him do. They manipulate. They're masters of it."

Riley stopped scrubbing and frowned at the putrid color of the shower wall. "How do you know that?"

"Because my dad was like that to my mom. I swore I'd never end up like him, but over the last two months, that's exactly where I landed. I'm sorry. You met my worst self."

"The baby—the cub—she's not yours, Drew. You know that, right? She's Bruiser and Diem's."

Drew waited a beat of silence before he said, "I know. I don't know why my animal went crazy like that. I've never had a problem being around Wyatt, and I don't have some wish for a cub of my own. I just..."

"Your instincts kicked in? Because of me?"

"Yeah. Something like that. Listen, I grabbed your duffle bag from Bruiser's truck and asked Diem what you've been craving, and she told me orange juice with crushed ice. The icemaker doesn't work in here, so I brought you a bucket of it from my place and some OJ." He cleared his throat. "Okay, I'm going to go. I'm sorry."

"That's the sweetest thing anyone's ever done for me," she blurted out, sticking her head back out the crack between the shower wall and the curtain.

Drew ducked back in the room. The smile on his lips was slow and only lifted one corner of his mouth, but it counted. Riley's heartrate raced. "I like when you smile. You should do it more often."

Drew arched his eyebrow and dipped his chin. "Keep giving me almost-peeks at those big old titties of yours, and I'll smile all you want."

Riley laughed and opened the curtain wide enough to splash him with water.

His laugh was deep and sexy as he pretended to look through the bigger space she'd created.

"Do you want to see my tummy?" she asked suddenly.

Heat flushed her cheeks, but he banished her embarrassment when the smile dipped from his lips and he nodded solemnly. "I do."

"I haven't shown anyone."

The smile returned just slightly. "Good." Approaching slowly, he reached for the curtain with his outstretched fingertips, then pulled it back.

With a squeak, she closed her eyes and stood ramrod straight, fists clenched at her sides. She'd never been this bold, but the need to show him all of her was something primal. She needed him to see her this way. The urge called to her from a place she'd forgotten existed. "Say something."

"Fuck it all, woman. You're beautiful."

She pursed her lips and exhaled shakily. When she opened her eyes, Drew was staring at her swollen breasts.

Nervously, she laughed. "My boobs are finally big, so it's only right I should show them to someone before they go away."

"They'll go away?"

"Mmm hmm. Within a few weeks of having Harper. Look, I know you didn't mean to show me your bear like that earlier, but I don't mind. I mean, I did at first, and I'm still a little shocked that I've met real life bear shifters, but... I guess what I'm trying to say is it's okay that you're different."

"Yeah?" His eyes met hers, trapped her in the hopefulness of his gaze.

"I got stretch marks."

His blond brows drew down, and he studied her stomach. "Where?"

She pointed to the little red rips on her stomach near her hips. "I made it to the last few weeks stretch mark free, and then these came in."

"Ahh, warrior stripes. That's what we call Brooke's when she fusses about them in a bathing suit. There's no shame in those," he said kneeling in front of the bathtub she was standing in. Gently, he gripped her waist in his oversize hands and brushed his lips against one mark and then the other.

Her breath shuddered when she felt the scratch of his two day scruff against her sensitive skin. "I like that. Warrior stripes," she murmured, brushing her hands through his hair. It was as soft as she'd imagined.

"My little warrior," Drew said low, kissing the first stretch mark again. "Selfless enough to give Diem and Bruiser a child and brave enough to stare down a crew of grizzly shifters." A kiss for the other mark again, and he rested his palms against her wet stomach, now alive with Harper's rolling movement. "Bruiser is one of my best friends, and he's going to make an amazing father. You're doing something incredible for him and his mate. Hell, for our whole crew. Babies are hard to come by for shifters. We don't breed easy."

"Do you want cubs someday?" she asked, stroking her fingers absently through the hair at his temples.

"You have shampoo in your hair," he whispered through a dazzling smile.

It wasn't lost on her that he'd avoided answering her question, but the hungry promise in his gaze made her train of thought derail completely.

"Will a shower hurt those cuts on your side?"

"If they do, I deserve the pain. I went after my friend tonight and scared you."

"In that case..." Riley poked her fingernail at his wounds, now half healed.

With a huffed laugh, he grabbed her wrist and angled away. "Woman, cut me a break, will you? I said I was sorry."

"Shower with me stranger-mate, for tonight has been incredibly strange and I need a shoulder massage. Oh, damn, I have to call my friend April back home and tell her I'm getting a shoulder massage from a sexy bear shifter."

Drew shucked his jeans as she ducked back behind the curtain to up the temperature of the water.

"You think I'm sexy?" he asked, a smile in his voice.

"You know you're sexy, so don't be one of those guys who needs compliments."

"That's a yes." The curtain opened and Drew stepped in with a giant erection jutting out between them.

"Holy shit," she murmured, eyes bulging.

"What, too small?" he asked through a smirk.

Riley snorted and ripped her gaze away from his long, thick shaft. Her middle was churning with need, and it had all started earlier today when he'd kissed her.

"Do you often kiss strangers?" she asked in a cultured accent.

"Only when they be as sexy as ye," Drew responded in a pirate voice.

Unable to help herself, she laughed. When he eased her under the jets of water and massaged her scalp gently, washing the suds away, she closed her eyes and groaned.

"I like your hair." His voice had gone soft and serious.

"Diem cut it. You like women with short hair then?"

"I like you."

Riley opened her eyes and clamped her hands around his wrists, stilling his hands against her hair. "I think if you really knew me, you wouldn't."

"Ahhh," he murmured, sounding unconvinced. "You have it all wrong. You'll figure out I'm a monster soon enough and run screaming for the hills. It's you who are too good to be with someone like me."

"I've seen your monster, remember? I've been with worse."

"Your ex?"

"You know what rhymes with ex?" she asked, desperate to change the subject.

"Tyrannosaurus Rex."

"Quit it. I'm trying to turn this conversation filthy," she said through a wicked grin. "Stop thwarting me."

"Thwarting?" he asked, eyebrows arched high. "Look around, woman. There ain't no need for that kind of language in the Asheland Mobile Park."

"Did you know," she said in a matter of fact tone, "that during pregnancy there is increased blood flow to the hoo-ha, and it makes nerve endings more reactive and sex more pleasurable?"

"Riley, if you're trying to seduce me with nerd shit, it's working."

"I Googled it."

Drew became very busy lathering up her washrag with a bar of soap. It wasn't until after he began gently washing her body, starting with her boobs of course, that he said, "I don't know if you're in the right frame of mind to sleep with me."

"I propose friends with benefits."

"Did you miss the part where my crazy-ass bear called you his mate? No. Sex is a bad idea."

Why did his rejection make her want to try harder? She was sucking at this whole seduction thing, but she hadn't been able to stop thinking about him since that kiss, and he was standing in front of her with his sexy dick all red and swollen and ready for her, and dammit, she hadn't even had the urge to touch herself in months, and now she was soaking herself just getting her nipples massaged by a washrag. So maybe she wasn't thinking straight, and perhaps she wasn't in the best emotional state after everything she'd learned tonight, but dammit, life was short. She wanted release, and she wanted Drew to give it to her.

A quickie shower bang with a sexy werebear sounded like just the medicine for what ailed her.

"Eat me," she said, light as air.

"Riley, stop it."

"I want you to touch me, Drew. Make me forget about the shit I'm dealing with and the crazy, *crazy* stuff I learned about the people here tonight. Make me forget everything. Please."

"I can't sleep with you, Riley. You slept with my best friend." Anger slashed across his ocean blue eyes before he looked away.

"What?" Okay, now she was utterly baffled. Last time she checked, she hadn't slept with anyone since Seamus. And that had been before he'd gone criminal. He had been drunk, popped a round in her, and rolled over, then began snoring immediately. Seamus hadn't been awesome at meeting her needs. Drew, undoubtedly would. "I haven't slept with anyone in over two years."

"Wait, then how are you pregnant with Bruiser's

child."

"Oooh," she drawled out. "No, Harper is one hundred percent Bruiser and Diem's baby. We did in vitro fertilization."

"What's that?"

"Well, doctors took one of Diem's eggs and Bruiser's sperm, put them on a blind date, then sent the little petri dish my way in a cooler, and then my doctor put the little baby in me. We got lucky, and the first one took. I mean, it was way more complicated than that, but there's the gist of it. This conversation has turned not-sexy, by the way."

"Disagree," Drew said, holding her against his body and spinning them so he was under the water. "I think it's sexy to get everything out in the open."

"Most guys would've been pounding me by now."

"I'm not most men," Drew said, shampooing his hair. "I like you. I want to take my time with you, savor you, talk, make you come before I do, taste you, touch you. But we're in a complicated situation, and I'm going to make damn sure you're ready for me, so I'm going to clear the air now with my intentions. I don't do friends with benefits. Not anymore. I do fuck me and you sleep beside me."

"Oh, my gosh," she drawled out, going all mushy. "You're a cuddler?"

"With you. I've wanted to hug you senseless all day, and if we're going to be intimate, I get that extra time with you. I want to big spoon you."

"I can live with that." Her round moon belly made it impossible to be anything but the little spoon. "Anything else?"

"Yes." He ran the bar of soap over his body, taking his time with his next negotiation. Leaning forward, he grazed his teeth over her neck playfully, then sucked on her bottom lip and left her swaying on her feet for more. "I want to take you out tomorrow morning."

"On a breakfast date?"

"Kind of, but not. I have plans."

Oh, this man was going to turn her into a puddle. "Anything else?" she squeaked out.

"Yeah, Tagan apparently planned this lame camping trip so we can all work our shit out before logging season begins. We leave in a couple of days, and we'll be back right before we go back to work on the landing. Now, I know you're heavy pregnant and you are probably uncomfortable and would be happier in Damon's temperature-controlled mansion, but I wanted to see if you wanted to go. With me. And everyone else, but mostly with me."

"Are you going to go all crazy-bear again if one of your crew gets too close?"

"Probably. My protective instincts are in beast-mode right now."

"If I asked you to try and control your bear, would you try?"

His eyes softened, and he pulled her close. "Of course, I will. You give me a good reason to not be like my father. Around you I feel…steadier."

Riley reached forward and traced a long, bulging vein down the side of his shaft. Drew shuddered. Emboldened by his instantaneous response, she slid her hand down him, from tip to base, until his eyes rolled and his head arched back. His sexy Adam's apple was so tempting to bite.

What the hell had come over her? She felt drunk on Drew already, just like she had when he'd kissed her earlier. Her mind was foggy with want as she slid her grip back up his erection.

Drew grabbed her hips and moved her backward until her back hit the cold plastic of the shower wall.

His dick brushed her stomach, and her belly contracted with need. Breath unsteady, she pulled another stroke and reveled in the growl that rattled Drew's throat. There was his bear, peeking out just enough that Drew's wild nature was exposed. Sure, she should probably be terrified right now, but damn, that noise was sexy.

Her breasts were tingling and aching now, but when Drew cupped one gently, the pain decreased. Dipping down, he pressed his lips on hers, lapping at her closed seam until she opened for him with a groan.

She rolled her hips, desperate to feel his skin against hers, but Harper was an epic cock shield right now.

"Holy moly, okay," she said between biting kisses. "How does this work. My stomach is in the way."

Drew chuckled patiently and nibbled at her earlobe before he whispered, "Let me worry about that."

He hit the tap behind him and folded her into his arms like she weighed less than air. It happened so fast, her stomach dipped. Wrapping her arms around his neck, she joked, "Thank goodness for your shifter strength."

"Stop it. You're perfect." Drew stepped out of the tub and toted her into the bedroom, then settled her gently on the bed.

"I'm all wet and slippery and look like a soggy marshmallow," she teased. "I'd make a fantastic Beluga whale shifter."

Drew knelt down, dragging her by the ankles to the edge of the bed. "I know you have more confidence than that." He grabbed the curve of her ass cheeks hard. "Tell me this isn't going to go away after you deliver."

"You like big butts?" Yeah, she was setting him up, but his cheeky smile said he wasn't falling for the game.

"I'm not finishing that lyric. You have the perfect ass." Drew dipped down and disappeared under the swell of her stomach. His teeth brushed her inner thigh, drawing gooseflesh from her ankles to pelvis.

"Oooh," she groaned out. "More of that." *Please, please, please!*

He kissed the peak of her wet folds and urged her legs wider with a steely grip on the back of her knees. His tongue flicked out and brushed against her clit, bowing her back against the bed. Oh, dear goodness, she was going to come too soon if he wasn't careful with the clever mouth of his. He sucked on her gently. Danger! Another lick, and she was toeing the edge.

"Drew," she gasped out. "I'm…" She was what? Fucking exploding, that was what.

Drew gripped her ass and pulled her hard against his mouth, slipping his tongue inside of her. A quick pulsing orgasm rocketed through her, and she cried out.

"Good woman," Drew murmured. "So sensitive for me."

And she was. This was better than any orgasm she'd had while not pregnant. The internet didn't lie, sa-weet!

Lights were sparking in the corners of her vision, and her hips jerked as Drew kissed her deeply with each aftershock, drawing every last one from her. He nibbled and sucked his way over the swell of her stomach, and Riley stifled the urge to pull the covers over them. She felt vulnerable after something so intimate and, finally sated from release, her thoughts were clearing. She was exposed, stretch marks and all. Perhaps she hadn't really thought this through... Oh! Drew clamped his lips over her nipple and sucked gently. That swollen, achy feeling was back as she arched against the mattress and cradled his head. With every stroke of his tongue, the pain lessened, but the pins and needles remained, giving her an erotic mix of pleasure and pain.

Drew jerked back, wide-eyed as he stared at her chest.

"What?" she asked, panicked.

Warmth trickled down her rib cage, and she frowned, then propped up on her elbows. To her mortification, a stream of white made a tiny river around the swell of her stomach and onto the comforter.

"Oh, no," she whispered in horror, reaching for the blanket. "I'm so sorry. That's never happened and—"

"That's fuckin' hot," Drew said on a breath, dragging his fingertip across the stream to break it. "Stop wiggling around and let me enjoy this. And put that cover down, woman. No hiding from me."

"But it's gross!" She felt like a cow whose udders

had gone too long without milking. "That's not supposed to happen until I deliver. Right?"

Drew gazed up at her, looking completely baffled. "I don't know. Maybe stimulation brings your milk sooner."

"Ugh, don't say that."

He cocked his head and grinned. "Milk. Milk, milk, milk, fucking awesome milk. Here let me do it to the other one."

"No! This is embarrassing enough."

"What? Why are you embarrassed? I'm not. Stop, Riley." He stilled her hand from pulling the comforter over her body. Resting his hand over her belly, he scooted closer beside her and tucked his arm under her head. Leveling her with the softest gaze, he said, "My dick is harder than it's ever been, and sharing that moment with you only made me want you more. I don't care what preconceptions you have about what's normal or not normal. Sex is natural. And sex during pregnancy has been going on for eons. I'm not the first man to draw a woman's milk from her."

"Swear it's not weird and you aren't going to go back to all your werebear friends and make fun of me tomorrow."

Drew snorted and leaned forward to brush his lips against hers. "That's not me, and even if you decided to tell everyone, I can guaran-damn-tee you what would happen. Brooke would tell you she and Tagan went through the same thing and that it's normal. Denison would make some crude joke and everyone would laugh with you, not at you, but then later he would ask me what sex with you being pregnant was like and want all the details. He and his mate, Danielle, are trying to get pregnant right now. And he has no filter."

With every word, Riley had relaxed. It might have been from his hand rubbing absently over the swell of her belly, but it was more likely from the fact that Drew was slowly making her realize this was okay. Body shaming herself wasn't going to do either one of them any good, and if the hard roll of Drew's dick against her leg was anything to go by, Drew really wasn't turned off by any of this. "You want to play with the other one?"

"Really?" Drew looked like a kid in a candy store.

"Yeah, really. It's probably sexier if I own it, right?"

"Well, I only get to play with you like this for a

couple more weeks, so yeah, Riley. Own that shit and let me get off on it."

She grinned mischievously. "Milk me."

Drew snickered and shook his head. "Eat me, Drew. Milk me, Drew," he said in soft, high-pitched notes before his voice deepened to his own again. "Demanding woman."

She shook her damp hair and stretched out languidly across the bed, comforter forgotten.

Drew rolled upward, then hovered over her, knees on either side of her hips and giant dick proudly on display. Oh, she liked this view.

His six pack abs flexed with every breath, and his eyes danced as he watched her. And that smile—the sexy, crooked smile that made the bottom drop out of her stomach—was back on his face. Flaxen tresses of his damp hair hung forward in front of his face as he settled his palms on the pillow on either side of her neck. Lowering slowly, he kissed her, plucking at her lips and teasing with his tongue. Then he moved his affection down her jaw to the base of her throat, and then in a trail between her full breasts. When he finally clamped his mouth over the nipple he hadn't played with yet, she reached forward and took a long stroke of his dick with her hand. Hot damn he was big, and swollen, and hard as a stone in her grip. And at the very tip was a drop of moisture that brought a delicious tremble up her spine. She wanted to taste it.

Drew rolled his hips, showing her the pace he liked. The tingling ache increased in her breast, and she bowed against him. His tongue lapped at her, drawing pleasure where there should've been discomfort. He smiled against her skin as the ache decreased and warmth streamed out of her. Easing back, he massaged her with his hand, pulling even more milk from her breast. He smeared it across her chest as his hips jerked harder with each of her strokes. His eyes lightened to that frosty gray, and his jaw clenched so hard, a muscle twitched and jumped there.

"I'm gonna come," he gritted out.

She released him immediately. That's not what she wanted. She didn't want him spilling onto her stomach when her sex was aching so badly for release with him.

"How do you want me?" she asked as soft as a breath.

The rattling growl was back in his throat as he

rolled his hips, almost as if he were still on the verge of release even without her touching him. "Roll over."

Okay, fuck yes, this was happening. She didn't like to be told what to do as a general rule, but when Drew, who was clearly as much animal as man right now, ordered her to do something in that sexy, growly voice of his? Well, she was just fine with minding him like this.

She flipped over faster than a pancake. He shoved a pillow under her hips and another under her breasts, and then told her, "Look up in that mirror right there, Riley. Watch me take you."

Her inner goddess was bouncing and clapping.

She drew her attention to the reflective glass over the dresser and stifled her natural urge to belittle herself. No make-up, damp hair drying in short waves, breasts swollen and pushed forward over the pillow, and still, Drew was looking at her reflection like she was the sexiest thing he'd ever laid eyes on. How could she feel anything less than beautiful with him looking at her like this? With him touching her like this?

He slid into her, inch by inch, until she was filled with him. His eyes closed, and a soft breath huffed from him as he grabbed her waist in a steely grip. She loved him like this. At the edge of his control. She'd done that—driven him wild.

He eased out, and then pushed into her again.

The pillow bumped her clit, sparking her sensitive nerve endings and pulling a soft gasp from her lips.

Drew spread her legs wider with his knee and slid into her again, harder this time.

His powerful hips pumped with every stroke. Riley couldn't pull her gaze away from their reflection if she tried. It was erotic to watch him take her from behind, but more than that, it was beautiful. Graceful. Powerful. He was taking her higher and higher, deeper into this overwhelming euphoria than she'd ever been before.

Drew growled, but it wasn't a threatening sound. It was a satisfied one that lifted gooseflesh on her back. He leaned forward, pressing his taut abs against her as he pumped into her. She met him stroke for stroke now, slamming back against him as the snarling grew louder. His teeth grazed her shoulder and she arched her back, crying out for more.

Release pounded through her as Drew froze

behind her, every muscle tensed. He grabbed her breast and gritted his teeth as his cock swelled inside of her, pumping warmth. Throbbing jets filled her, and she closed her eyes at how blindingly good he felt connected to her like this.

Drew's eyes, almost snow-colored in the dim light from the bathroom, held her trapped in the mirror. "I understand the cub is not," he said in an odd, growly voice, "but you, Riley...you're mine."

NINE

"Well, that escalated quickly." Riley sipped the glass of orange juice Drew had handed her and stifled a groan. Pulp free and everything, just how she liked it. Drew was racking up the points with her tonight.

He chuckled from beside her on the bed. Riley was sitting against the creaking headboard, while Drew was lying down with his feet dangling off the end, gloriously naked and propped up on his elbow near her stomach. He hadn't taken his eyes off Harper's rolling movement for the last five minutes, and his hand drifted gently over Riley's tummy to wherever the movement was.

"In my defense, I tried to slow us down," he murmured.

True.

Her body felt like a noodle after what they'd done, but not in a bad way. She was practically glowing from the inside out as warmth and happiness radiated from her. It wasn't even possible to remember the last time she felt this safe.

Stroking his hair gently, she sighed and wished this moment could stretch for eternity.

"Will it be hard after you deliver Harper?" he asked.

"You mean will it hurt?"

"No. Will it be hard for you to give her up?"

She sucked in air at the pain his question caused. She hadn't talked about this, hadn't admitted it out loud, and for good reason. But talking to Drew made things better. Not in the way talking through this process with her counselor had done either. Telling him about her fears would be sharing them with Drew, not dumping them on him and leaving. Someone else, someone stronger, could help her carry the weight.

With a deep, steadying exhalation, she looked

down at the part of her stomach where Harper had decided to kick repeatedly. "Yes, it'll be hard. I try not to think about it. Every time I do, my mind skitters away from the thought of how it will be handing her to Diem and watching another woman bond with the baby I love so much. My counselor said that maybe it would be best for me not to see Harper at all, and I think she's right. I don't want to fall in love with her even more. Diem and Bruiser wanted those 3D sonograms taken of her, just so they could feel like part of the process, and I sent them in the mail without taking a single peek. I haven't looked at any of the ultrasounds either."

"You don't want to see her at all? Even after she's born?"

Riley shook her head sadly. "She's not mine to keep, so I don't want to bond with her any more than I already have."

Drew dragged his attention away from Riley's undulating stomach and looked up at her, a knit of worry in his brows. "If it's so hard, why are you doing this?"

Diem's explanation whispered through Riley's mind. *Redemption.*

"I told you if you knew me, you wouldn't like me," she whispered, throat tightening around the words. "I killed someone. Giving Diem and Bruiser a child feels like the only way I can make up for what I've done."

Drew sat straight up and pulled her against his chest hard. "Tell me."

"My ex, Seamus, was a bad man. I didn't know it when we were dating. I knew he had a dark, brooding side and that his friends were crazy, but he did a really good job of hiding who he really was from me. But the darker parts of him began eking out about a year after we'd started dating. He'd get a call and leave late at night. I thought he was cheating, but one night I found a bloody rag in our bathroom trashcan. And while he was sleeping, I searched him all over for the cut that had caused it. Maybe it was a bloody nose, but I just had this feeling it wasn't his blood. I found a gun hidden at the bottom of a laundry basket once, and police came by asking where he was on two separate occasions. Seamus wasn't at my apartment either time, so I didn't have to lie when I told them I didn't know where he was. I should've left him then. Should've bowed out and accepted I was in over my head, but he'd done such a good job of keeping whatever he was doing separate from me and the life we were building together."

Riley swallowed hard as she was bombarded with memories of that night. "We were supposed to go out dancing at this new club downtown, and I'd dressed up for him. He was late, and I was so mad he was standing me up again, but he finally showed up around midnight. He wasn't alone, though. He was with one of his friends, and they were pulling in this man with tape over his mouth. He was wearing a business suit, and his hair was all mussed. His cheek was split and bleeding, and when he made noises behind the tape, he sounded scared. Really scared. I went ballistic. Why had they brought him into my apartment? Seamus and his friend were caked in sweat, and Seamus's eyes looked crazy. He kept repeating, 'He saw it. He saw too much.' Seamus made a phone call in the other room while his friend tied the man to a chair in my kitchen. I should've called the police then, but I didn't. I don't know why. I was so pissed and not thinking straight, and I wanted them to let the man go and get out of my apartment. Seamus's friend left, and I overheard my ex tell him he'd 'take care of it.' I was hysterical, crying, asking questions. Something was wrong, and what was happening didn't feel like my life. I'd never even gotten a speeding ticket, and now the scene in my kitchen was straight out of some terrifying cop show. Seamus told me to get out. I screamed at him, and he slapped me. Just once, right across the cheek. I was stunned and stood there, frozen. He told me to get out and stay with my friend April for the night. And I did. I just left. That man was watching me leave, his last chance, with scared eyes, and I just ran out of there like I had no courage at all. I took a bus all the way to April's house, sobbing like a lunatic the whole way before I snapped out of it. I called the police from her front lawn, but when they got to my apartment, it was already too late."

"Seamus killed him?"

Riley blinked rapidly, trying to contain the tears that were blurring her vision as she nodded. "I testified against him. Gave the courts everything I could ever remember about Seamus and answered every question about that night. I didn't keep anything to myself, but it didn't bring that man back. Turns out, he wasn't involved in crime like Seamus and his friends. He was just some guy who witnessed too much on his walk from work to his house where his wife and two young daughters lived. His family was in the courtroom. I apologized to them after the trial. I should've done more, faster. Should've thrown a massive fit and cut him loose, not gone spineless the second Seamus had slapped me."

"You didn't kill that man, Riley. Seamus did. You brought his family justice by calling the cops and testifying against him."

April had said the same thing. Over and over, she'd tried to convince her it wasn't her fault, but it hadn't ever sunk in. Riley couldn't help but blame herself for those two little girls growing up without a father. For the wife who probably had cried herself to sleep at nights, missing the man she loved.

"They let him out, you know. He was convicted, and now he's out on parole. It doesn't make any sense. Someone pulled some big strings to release him. I was a wreck after he got locked up, and the only thing that calmed me after the nightmares was the idea of doing something really good for someone to make up for what I'd done to that family. When I researched surrogacy, I knew I was a terrible candidate, but I was healthy and determined, and I found Diem and Bruiser. And the second the doctor told me I had a viable pregnancy for them, I knew I'd made the right choice. I felt...not like my old self...but like I could bear myself again. Like someday, I might be okay."

"You will be, Riley," Drew murmured against her hair. "I promise. You've taken a great deal of guilt onto your shoulders that you didn't need to." His lips pressed against her temple, lingered there. "You're a very brave woman, you know that? I could sense it in you from the moment I met you, but hearing what you've gone through makes me realize it even more. To testify against someone you're scared of?" He shook his head respectfully. "I'm so proud of you."

Riley exhaled a long, shaky breath, releasing some of her fear and tension along with it. God, it felt so good to hear those words. To hear he didn't hate her for what had happened. The trial had been public, and reactions from the city she lived in all over the board. But she'd exposed her grief and the awful details of that night, and Drew hadn't flinched away from her. He'd called her brave instead.

"Your turn," she whispered. "Who did you lose to

make your bear go mad?"

Drew went rigid against her and didn't answer. Minutes ticked by, and she thought he wouldn't respond at all, but at last he said, "My mom."

"Momma's boy?"

"Always."

"How did she die?"

His breath hitched in his chest. "In an assisted care facility. Alone. Riley, I can't..."

"You should. Keeping it inside will only poison you. I would know."

With a snarl, Drew rocketed off the bed and strode from the room. Riley sat there wide-eyed and stunned as the front door slammed. Moments later, it creaked open again and Drew appeared at the bedroom door, anger slashing across his lightening eyes.

"Fuck," he muttered, ripping his gaze away from her. He stared at the floor as he said, "My dad was a grade-A, pure-as-they-come, raging asshole. He was also a giant grizzly shifter."

"Is that why your grizzly is so much bigger than Bruiser's?"

"Yeah. Except he didn't use his size to scuffle

with other males in his crew. He used it on my mom."

"Shit," she breathed in horror. She'd been slapped by Seamus once, and it had haunted her, feeling so helpless, being treated like dirt. She couldn't imagine a woman having to go through that on a regular basis.

"You didn't kill anyone, Riley. You think you did, but you didn't. I have."

"Your father?"

"Yep. He went after my mom really bad one night right after my eighteenth birthday, and I lost it. She was just lying there...fuck. Riley?" he said, lifting his eyebrows in a warning glare.

"Say it and be done with it, Drew. It's just me. I'll hold your secrets."

"I killed him, and we went to trial. Someone hired an expensive lawyer. One of those who never loses, no matter what the defendant has done. Later I found out it was Damon Daye who'd paid all the lawyer fees. After what my dad had done to my mom, it was called self-defense, and I was released. My mom was a human, and my dad hurt her so bad, it damaged her mind. Her brain. Swelling...shit. She lived the rest of her life in assisted living while I worked here to pay for the nurses and doctors and medicines and care for her. I visited every two days, and sometimes she would remember me and sometimes she wouldn't. Her life was ruined by my dad, but I tried to make her last years as happy as I could. Birthday parties in her room, Christmas, mother-son dances. I checked her out of that place any time the doctors told me she was stable enough, and me and one of her nurses would take her to the park because she loved..." Drew's face crumpled, and he scrubbed his hand down his jaw as the first tear slipped down his face. "She loved the ducks. She loved feeding them. It was one of the few times I could get a smile from her, and I lived for that." Drew inhaled deeply and sauntered over to the bed, sat beside Riley and put his hand over her stomach where Harper had gone still. "Her main doctor said I had to stop seeing her so much because she had seizures when I would leave. I was getting her too excited with my visits, and he wanted her to even out and stabilize before I went back to my normal visitation. She passed away two months ago when I wasn't there. They buried her in the cemetery in Saratoga, but I haven't been able to visit yet."

"Why?"

"I don't have a headstone on her grave yet. They're expensive, and I'm buckling under her leftover medical bills. It'll be easier when logging season starts and I'm earning a steady paycheck again, but I want to pay off everything and get her a really pretty headstone, and I want to tell her that everything is taken care of and she can rest easy and not worry about me."

"Oh, Drew," Riley said, wrapping her arms around his shoulders and hugging him up tight. "I'm so sorry."

He huffed an emotional laugh. "You know, she would've loved you."

"I wish I could've met her."

Drew turned and smiled, but it didn't reach his eyes. "I swear I see her sometimes out in the woods. Just a flash of her, smiling like she used to before my dad...and then she's gone. Just poof." He snapped. "Like that. There, now you can see how crazy I really am."

"You're not crazy. You just miss her."

He leaned forward and kissed her, his lips going soft against hers. "You hungry?" he asked when he eased away.

"Nice subject change."

"Thank you. Is that a yes?"

"I'm always hungry."

"Good, because I'm not going to be able to sleep for a while after all of that, and I like to cook when I'm up like this. You want to see my trailer?" He waggled his eyebrows, and she could imagine how he'd dealt with the heaviness of his life before his mother had passed away. With jokes and laughter to detract from the pain he was hiding inside.

"I want meat," she said through a slow grin.

"Thata girl. Put your clothes on and let me feed you."

Just like that, Drew had admitted his darkest secrets and thoughts, and in the next instant, had offered to care for her.

That's what Drew was, a caregiver. Focusing on his own pain obviously didn't ease his ache. Taking care of someone else did—her sweet, protective bear.

And Riley's heart tethered to him a little more.

TEN

"A flea market?" Riley yelled, clasping her hands in front of her chest.

Drew hunched down, drawing his shoulders to his ears as he turned into the field that served as a parking lot. "Damn, woman, with the yelling. My ears are more sensitive than yours."

"Oh, right. Bear ears. Sorry." She lowered her voice to a whisper-scream. "A flea market?"

He chuckled, practically beaming at her response to their morning date. "There's a lady who runs one of these booths who specializes in old worn-out furniture. I want to buy you a piece if you find something you like."

Riley peeled herself from the window and said, "You're trying to make me fall in love with you, aren't you?"

"Hell yeah."

The brakes squeaked as he pulled up next to a white minivan with a plethora of kids filing out of it.

"Wait, what about breakfast. I'm hungry."

"The steak and eggs at two this morning weren't enough to tide you over?" The grin on his face said he was teasing, but she swatted him anyway.

"I'm eating for two. I'm hungry all the time. Plus, my morning sickness lasted forever, and I'm just now able to enjoy food again."

"Open your door and take a sniff."

She did, and the scent of cinnamon and sugar immediately brought a growl to her stomach. "Cinnamon rolls?"

"Yep. Our first stop."

She let off a tiny squeal, more careful of his oversensitive hearing this time, then leaned over and pecked him on the lips. "Today is the best."

His answering smile nearly stopped her heart.

After locking up his old truck, Drew led her

toward the farthest booth where a crowd was already gathered. Riley slipped her hand into his. Butterflies flapped around her stomach when he looked down at her.

"You're killin' me today," Drew said.

"Why?"

"Because you're so damned cute."

Hmm. Her face was probably going to hurt from smiling by the end of this.

They stood in line for cinnamon rolls, which were burn-your-fingers hot and served in thick paper wrapping. Frosting oozed everywhere, but Riley didn't care. Drew made her comfortable, and twice he leaned in and sucked the sweetness from her lips. It was hard to be self-conscious around a man who was so amused with everything she said and did.

Drew talked animatedly between gooey bites of his own breakfast about the art of lumberjacking. He told her about the skyline and the processor, how they hauled the trees up by threes, and who manned which machine. He talked about the shit he got into with the Ashe Crew, and she made a mental note to play a game called beer pong after Harper arrived. As they meandered from booth to booth, he told her about how each woman had come to join the Ashe Crew, but in a way that hid their shifter identities by anyone passing by in the crowded market.

Drew couldn't seem to stop touching her. A hand on her back here, fingertips on her cheek there, a sipping kiss at a booth that sold carved figurines. Drew bought her a wooden bear that was so small, she could carry it around in her pocket.

By the time they made their way to the furniture booth, Drew had been telling her funny stories for an hour, and now she felt like she knew each and every one of the Ashe Crew. And in a strange twist, she was actually missing them, and excited about the camping trip when she'd get to know the crew better. It didn't matter that Harper was going to be raised in a trailer park out in the middle of nowhere. She was going to grow up with the strongest, most incredible role models.

"Where'd you get those eyes?" Drew asked as she knelt down by an old chair with a broken lancet arch and a hole where the seat should've been.

"From both my parents. My mom is from the Philippines, and my dad is a green-eyed Irishman. Their mixed genetics did something weird with me."

"Not weird. Beautiful. It's hard to look away from you."

Riley scrunched up her nose. "Kids in school used to say I looked funny."

"Ha!" Drew leaned down and whispered in her ear. "My chronic boner says you don't look weird."

Riley giggled and bit his neck gently. "I want this chair, but I want to pay for it."

"This one? It's broken, though. What about that pair back there," he said, pointing deeper into the booth. "Those look like they're in good shape."

"But what's the fun in that? I like fixing broken pieces. Someone else would just throw this piece away, but I can make it beautiful and useful again. I can make it a feature in someone's home." She was already ticking off a list in her head of what she would need to refurbish the chair and give it an updated look that would have customers clambering for it on her website. Perhaps a soft gray paint and distress to keep the rustic feel. She'd need to find the right material to reupholster the seat, but that would be fun, shopping the fabric store in Saratoga for the perfect one. When she looked up, Drew was standing again, but he was looking at her with the most curious, adoring expression.

"What?" she asked through a shy smile.

"You're just...remarkable. I shouldn't even be surprised that you picked the rattiest chair here to fix up."

"Remarkable." She dipped her voice low. "There ain't no room in this here trailer park for words like that."

He snorted a laugh and flipped over the price tag on the arm of the chair. "We'll take this one," he told a woman sitting beside the booth wall, reading a book with a steamy romance cover. Drew handed her a twenty dollar bill and didn't even haggle.

"Wait, I wanted to pay for it. You have a lot to pay for already with your mom's medical bills."

Hoisting the chair gently with one hand, Drew pulled Riley against his side, and then his arm over her shoulder. He leaned into her and pulled her earlobe between his teeth, then released her. Oh, what that man did to her insides.

"Let me do something nice for you," he murmured. "Earlier, you said today is the best. Well, it is for me, too. Talking to you about everything last night made me feel better. Made my bear feel less unruly. You did that for me." He was whispering against her ear now, revving up her hormones into a frenzy, when he went still and rigid beside her, jerking them to a stop.

"What's wrong?" she asked.

He twisted and looked behind them, then muttered a curse and spun them around to face a trio of wide-shouldered, powerhouse men who were headed their way.

"Kong," Drew greeted the biggest. His voice had lost all humor.

The titan crossed his arms over his chest, tree-trunk arms flexing with the motion. "Beast."

Tension sparked in the air between the two men, so Riley stepped forward, hand extended. "I'm Riley."

Kong looked at her palm, then at her belly, encased in a skin-hugging tan sweater. "I know who you are. That's the reason we came over here."

"What?" Riley said, dropping her hand to her side.

"Look," Kong said, swinging his attention to Drew. "I'm not pissed you kicked my ass. It was a good fight, and I respect you and your crew. I know you've been around in this community for a long time, and hell, my crew even likes going to Sammy's and watching Dennison and Brighton play. Because I respect your crew and in the interest of staying on Damon Daye's good side, I wanted to give you a warning."

"What warning?" Drew asked low.

"A man's been staying at the hotel in town and asking around about a woman with dark hair, green eyes, and pregnant. He caught up to a couple of my boys at Sammy's last night and showed them a picture. Asked if my crew had seen her." Kong swung his dark gaze to Riley, heavy eyebrows lowered. "It was you in that picture."

"Seamus," she said on a terrified breath.

Kong ran his hand through his short hair and gave her a sympathetic look. "I wouldn't want nothin' to happen to you or that baby you're carrying. Be wary, yeah?"

Drew shook the giant's hand and thanked him, then stood stock still, watching them as they left. "How'd he find you?"

"He must've followed the bus routes and figured out where I stopped. There were only three that left that night from Minneapolis, so maybe he found out which one I took and tracked me to Saratoga." The world was spinning, and she swayed on her feet. Seamus was here, in Saratoga. "He's hunting me." Her voice came out small and weak, and she hated how fragile that man made her feel. "He's out on parole, but I have an active restraining order against him."

"That's ballsy, him out in public like that trying to find you even when you have a restraining order."

Ballsy, or the man had a superiority complex that made him feel like he was invincible. Prison had warped what little of his mind he had left.

"We should go," she said, suddenly feeling watched. Out of all of the passersby in the marketplace, the odds of Seamus having talked to some of them were huge.

"Yeah," Drew said, guiding her between two booths toward the field he'd parked the truck in.

She was in full-blown panic mode by the time they reached the pickup. Throat tightening, breath hitching, frantically scanning for danger, hugging her precious middle. Gads, Seamus had been fast tracking her down.

Drew set the chair in the bed of the truck and opened her door, then helped her in. Something above her senses was emanating from Drew and electrifying the hairs on her arms. When his eyes met hers, they were that wild and unsettling snowy color. "I won't let him hurt you. I swear it, Riley. You're still safe. I'm going to take you home—"

"Home?"

"To ten-ten, and then I'm going to gather some of the boys, and we'll take care of Seamus."

"Drew, this isn't your fight."

"The hell it is! Murderer doesn't care about a restraining order, doesn't care about harassing a woman who is pregnant," he said, ticking each off with his fingers. "Stalker who laid hands on you. Riley, I know you can take care of yourself. I *know* you can." Drew cupped her cheeks. "But you have Harper, and we can't just wait for him to come find you."

"Yes, we can."

Drew's determined face faltered. "What do you mean?"

Seamus was here for her, and the Ashe Crew didn't need any extra human attention on them. Did she appreciate Drew's offer to save her? Hell yes. But if she was going to find the person she used to be again, she had to save herself. "I have a plan."

ELEVEN

Sammy's bar was busy for a Sunday night. It was a non-smoking bar, but that didn't stop the occasional odd look she got from the townies, likely because she was about a hundred months pregnant in a drinking establishment.

Riley shook her hands out and reminded herself for the tenth time that Drew was sitting at the bar watching her inconspicuously. And so was Bruiser, Tagan, and Kellen. And also some of the Gray Backs, whom Drew introduced her to, and a lone Boarlander named Harrison. And Skyler and Everly were playing pool in the corner, watching her like hawks...er...like a falcon and a bear. Now that she thought about it, there weren't very many humans in here. She couldn't predict the future, but if Seamus tried anything, she imagined her new friends would rip him a new asshole—literally.

She took another sip of her orange juice and crushed ice and smiled at the fact that Drew had asked her three times today if she was craving anything he could get for her. Doting bear. Was it possible to fall in love with someone after knowing them for such a short time? She hadn't really believed in love at first sight, but now she was second guessing everything. No one in her lifetime had come close to affecting her like Drew did.

She cast another nervous glance at Drew, but he crossed his eyes and gave her a goofy smile. With a giggle, she sucked down the last of her juice and stood. They'd been here for forty-five minutes already, and her bladder was currently on a forty-minute timer.

After a quick piddle party, she looked in the bathroom mirror and pursed her lips in disappointment at the fear she saw in her own eyes. She was stronger than this. Lifting her lip, she snarled like she'd heard Drew and the other bear shifters do when he'd gone to the Ashe Crew with the truth of why she'd run away from Minneapolis. The human-sounding noise that rattled up her throat didn't sound very threatening, but it sure made her feel braver.

The door opened and Drew stepped through, then locked the door behind him.

"What are you doing?"

"You," he ground out, approaching in two long strides.

He lifted the hem of the gray, skin-tight sweater dress Brooke had let her borrow from her old stash of maternity clothes and pressed Riley against the bathroom wall.

"I hate that he's going to be this close to you," Drew gritted out as he pushed her panties to the side.

He captured her lips with his and brushed his tongue against hers. "Can you come fast for me?"

With a needy sound, she bit his bottom lip and nodded.

Drew cupped her sex, then slid his finger into her. His palm brushed her clit just right, as if he'd already learned her body. Her breath hitched as she wrapped her arms tighter around his neck and rolled her hips with every stroke. Warm tendrils stretched from between her legs to her middle as pressure built with every thrust of his finger. When he added a second, she was gone. He caught her cry with his mouth, kissing her hard and swallowing down the sound of her pleasure.

He kissed her once, twice, before his lips went soft. His jaw moved as he sipped her, tasted her, adored her. And when the last of her aftershocks had subsided, he put her panties back into place and straightened the hem of her dress. She leaned heavily on the wall like a tranquilized moose while he washed his hands with a cocky smirk. Before he left, he kissed her on the cheek and said, "Kong called. They're bringing Seamus now. He'll be here in five minutes. Oh," he said, turning back at the door, "you look fucking beautiful tonight. That dress, woman." He shook his head and grinned like she'd undone him. Then he spun and left her noodle-legged in the bathroom.

By the time she stumbled her way back to the table where a new orange juice was waiting for her, she was ready to face down Seamus so she could hurry and go back to ten-ten and beg some cuddles from Drew, who had proved last night he was awesome at them. Plus, he'd promised her a foot massage when she'd complained on the way over to Sammy's about her heels hurting.

Two minutes later, Kong walked through the door, followed by one of the men she'd seen him with at the flea market, and Seamus.

His soulless eyes were dark as night and narrowed to slits as he searched the bar for her. His crop of unruly dark hair looked unwashed, and a three day beard shadowed his jaw. Winter blasted through her veins when his empty eyes landed on her.

You can do this.

Careful not to look at her friends, she let her terror show on her face and stood. "What are you doing here?" she hissed out as he approached.

He jammed his finger at her chair and ordered her to "Sit." Like she was a fucking Doberman. What had she ever seen in him?

Slowly, she lowered herself to the chair. Seamus took his seat and spun it backward, then slammed it down onto the cracked concrete floor. "I bet you thought you were safe from me, didn't you? I told you I'd find you, you little cunt. You're mine. That baby is mine—"

"No, she isn't," Riley gritted out. "I'm a surrogate, you idiot, just like I've told you. I'm having this baby for someone else."

"Horseshit!" he yelled. Looking around, he lowered his voice. "I came here to get my family back."

"I'm not your family, Seamus. We're done. We were done the day you brought that poor man into my apartment and made me a part of murder—"

"And I said I was sorry for that in the letters I sent you from prison."

"I didn't read your letters, Seamus! I testified against you. Do you not remember that? How could you not think we're over when I was the one who worked the hardest to put you behind bars? I'm not yours. I never really was. Please let me go."

Seamus slammed his palms down on the table and donned an empty smile. Leaning back, he dragged his hands over the smooth metal surface and shook his head. "You still love me."

"I don't."

"You do."

"Oh, for fuck's sake, I'm not having this argument. I hope you can move on with your life," she said, standing. "I hope you can try to make up for the harm you've done somehow, but I will never, ever be a part of your life again."

Riley spun on her heel and strode for the hallway that led past the bathroom and to a back exit. Drew's truck was parked in the back parking lot.

A steely grip clamped around her arm and shoved her backward against a wall. "Don't you walk away from me again, Ri," Seamus said, his breath hot against her face.

She whimpered and closed her eyes as she tried to escape his lips. Pushing against him as hard as she could, she jerked her knee upward and caught him in the groin the second his mouth touched hers.

Seamus's weight disappeared, and he slammed into the opposite wall so hard the sheetrock caved in. Drew was there, hunched in front of her, shifting his weight from side to side with the grace of a panther. His hand was behind him, resting on her stomach, but she was all right. Harper, too, if the ninja-kicks going on in her belly were anything to go by.

"We're okay," she murmured, grasping his hand just to feel safe again.

Drew lurched forward so fast he blurred. He caught Seamus around the neck and lifted him off the floor.

"Drew," Tagan barked out. "Let him go. The police are on their way.

Seamus was struggling now, turning red in the face and making choking sounds, his boots kicking desperately, hitting the wall in a rhythmic *clunk, clunk, clunk.*

"We took pictures of everything," Tagan said. "Me, Bruiser, Skyler...three separate camera phones with proof that this asshole followed her across state lines and stalked her to this bar. And Kong has already said he and his men will make statements about how aggressively he was looking for Riley. He's going back to jail where he can't hurt her. Drop him."

"Drew," Riley murmured, sliding a hand up his tensed back. "Let him go. Let the police have him."

He stood frozen for the span of three heartbeats, then cast Seamus to the floor like a ragdoll. The growl that emanated from him was intimidating enough, but when he turned, his eyes were almost white.

"Oh, no," she whispered.

Dragging him deeper into the hallway, back where the fluorescent lights didn't reach, she pulled him to her. He buried his head against her shoulder, hiding his eyes from the crowd gathering in the hallway, and hugged her tightly. She didn't have to worry about Seamus. When she looked over at the commotion at the other end of the hall, Bruiser had him pinned down. Sirens wailed in the distance.

"I can't," Drew gritted out in a strange voice.

"You can't what?"

"I have to Change."

She shoved open the back exit, but flashing red and blue lights blinded her. Riley pulled the door closed again and rubbed her cheek against his in an affectionate gesture she'd seen the Ashe Crew do with their mates. "You can't Change now. Bear, I need Drew for a while longer. I *need* him." She eased back and kissed him softly. "Please."

The growling softened, and moments later, Drew's shoulders relaxed under her palms and he rested his forehead against hers. His eyes were dimming by the second, and by the time the door was thrown open by the police, he looked human once again.

He'd controlled his animal tonight as he'd said he would for her. He'd already changed from the out-of-control brawler who had attacked Bruiser that first night. But more than that, he'd trusted her to come in here tonight and fight beside him, not behind him.

"You did so well," she whispered.

Drew looked utterly exhausted, but he mustered a small smile. "My brave mate. So did you."

TWELVE

A knock sounded on the door, and Riley stopped tucking her extra pair of maternity jeans into a backpack Drew had given her. This wasn't like when she'd packed to leave Minneapolis. The knock was much more polite than Seamus's had been, and now she was packing for something fun—the camping trip.

"Come in!" she called out.

The screeching of the door sounded, then heavy footsteps headed her way. Tagan poked his head in with an easy smile. "Hey, Brooke wanted me to bring these by." He held up a stack of clothes. "It'll be chilly, so she wanted you to have lots of options on what to bring."

Riley beamed. "Your wife is awesome, you know that?"

"Yeah," he said with a chuckle. "I got lucky. Hey, listen. I actually wanted to say something to you, so I kind of jacked my mate's care package for the excuse."

"Tagan, you're alpha here. I know I don't understand all of the dynamics, but Drew has explained a lot of them to me, and I'm trying to learn. I know you run this place. You don't need an excuse to talk to me."

He strode into the bedroom and set the clothes beside her backpack on the bed. "I think what you're doing for Bruiser and Diem is really noble."

"I'm doing it to make up for something awful—"

"Doesn't matter, Riley. Nothing matters to me before the day you arrived here. What matters is what you do with your life from here on. If you got mixed up in something, at least you're trying to make up for it. How many people would do that? Not many. Most would chock it up to life experience and move on. You're a complicated woman. Sensitive to things other people don't feel. You demanding to be a part of getting Seamus back behind bars last night is a testament to how strong you are. You could've let us handle it—"

"But then human attention would have been on your crew if you just beat the shit out of him, Tagan."

"Exactly," he said in a soft voice. "I have to think of those things because the survival of my crew depends on my ability to put my animal instincts away and make rational decisions for us. You did that last night without me explaining anything to you. If you were a bear, I'd say you would make a great alpha someday."

"Really?" Tears stung her eyes, and she blinked to clear her blurry vision.

Tagan lifted his chin and sighed. "I also wanted to thank you for helping to get Drew back under control last night. He's had a rough go of it lately."

"I know, and you're welcome. He's important to me. I'm assuming him Changing in that tiny hallway wasn't the way you planned on coming out to the public?"

"Ha! No. Drew will not be our poster boy for coming out. His bear is a bit of a beast to handle. Not around you, though, for some odd reason." A knowing smile spread across Tagan's face, landing in his bright blue eyes. "I know you have a life back where you came from, but I want to extend an invitation for you to stay."

"For how long?"

"Forever. Drew is acting more like himself around you, and a part of me—" Tagan's voice cracked with emotion, and he cleared his throat before he continued. "A part of me thought we wouldn't see this side of him again. The alpha before me, Jed, went mad. His bear took him down a path he couldn't come back from, and I was scared Drew's animal was going to accomplish the same thing. You stopped that freefall, Riley. You feel...important here."

Riley opened her mouth to say she couldn't, that when Harper was born, she'd have to leave. She didn't think she could handle watching the baby bond with her real parents, but she couldn't come up with the words to reject him after such a generous offer. "I'll think about it," she murmured instead.

Sadness washed through Tagan's blazing eyes, as if he could hear the lie in her voice. Perhaps bear shifters could. She didn't know.

"All right, I'll see you out front. We're leaving in ten minutes. Will you be ready by then?"

"Yeah, I just have to pack some extra snacks, and I'll be out there."

Tagan left, and the ache of a loss she didn't understand spread through her like a fog. She should feel great right now after his uplifting words. He seemed like the type of man who gave his respect only to those who deserved it, and he'd given it to her. But he'd also brought up the realization that she was full-term, due to deliver in two weeks, and after that, she'd be leaving.

It suddenly seemed way too soon. Two weeks wasn't long enough to live a lifetime of memories in this place.

Baggies of fruit, cheese cubes, honey roasted peanuts, and crackers gathered, Riley zipped up the backpack and slung it over her shoulder, determined to ditch the melancholy thoughts so she could enjoy today. She'd never been camping before.

When she stepped out of 1010, an immediate grin stretched her face. The trailer park was in chaos right now. Kellen stood near Denison's Bronco with a giant bird latched onto his arms by long, curved talons. Skyler was an intimidating size. From the animal magazines she'd read as a child, she didn't remember falcons being that big. Skyler stretched her wings to keep her balance as Kellen reached out to clap Denison on the back. Danielle, his human mate, was filling a small water trough and trying to get a little gray pygmy goat to stop chewing on the bottom hem of her jeans. The others were running here and there, packing up the back of a big, black, lifted truck with coolers, tents, bag chairs, and other camping supplies she didn't have a guess at. Drew was leaned up against the bed of Bruiser's truck, talking to him with a lingering smile in his eyes. Damn it was good to see him happy after last night, and it was even better seeing him talk so easily with Bruiser again. There wasn't any of the tension she'd sensed in them the night they had fought.

When Drew saw her, he grinned big and jogged over to her. "Let me get that," he murmured, pulling the backpack from her shoulder. "We're going to ride with Bruiser, Kellen and Diem. Skyler's going to find us a good spot to camp from the air. Damn, woman," he said, raking his gaze down the thick, red sweater she wore and her dark wash jeans. Drew climbed the last stair that stood between then and kissed her gently. "I missed you."

Riley sighed happily and wrapped her arms around his neck. "You just saw me an hour ago," she teased. "What's going to happen when you start work at the landing in a few days and have to spend entire days away from me?"

Drew kissed her harder, biting her lip as a tiny punishment. "No more talk of being apart." He wrenched his voice up an octave and impersonated her. "Today is the best!"

Giggling, she swatted his arm and followed him down the stairs toward Bruiser's truck.

One bench seat in a single cab truck was not going to hold three full-grown grizzly shifters, a dragon shifter, and a pregnant human, but when Kellen tossed Skyler up into the air and watched her fly off, then hopped into the bed of the truck with Drew, it was clear.

Diem climbed in beside Bruiser, and Riley took the window seat. Drew opened a sliding rear window and gave her a wink. Dadgum, he looked sexy. Those long, powerful legs encased in jeans that hung just right on him, heavy hiking boots, a white thermal sweater that clung to his physique so tightly she could see every muscular curve of his shoulders and pecs. His shoulder-length blond hair was flipped to the side and messy in that sexy, just-got-out-of-bed look, and his blue eyes were practically dancing with happiness. And that smile...holy hell, that crooked, cocky smile was going to be the death of her.

She grinned at him and felt like the luckiest woman on earth to have caught his attention.

And she'd be leaving soon.

Dragging her attention to the front window so he wouldn't see the pain that thought had caused her, she made a silent promise to herself. For the trip, she wouldn't think about the end to what had turned out to be the happiest time in her life. She would live in the here and now and enjoy being with the man she was falling in love with, future complications be damned.

Tagan was driving the lead truck and followed Skyler for about an hour before they all pulled into a clearing where she landed on a mossy tree trunk.

"Aw, this is perfect," Bruiser muttered, leaning forward to stare up at the thick canopy of pine limbs above them. Along the clearing was a gently rolling river, and the ground was smooth and level. All around them, the woods were alive with the sound of late season birds.

Drew opened her door, then helped her and Diem out. His hand was warm when he slipped it around Riley's and led her toward the river with the rest of the Ashe Crew. They stood on the edge looking over the body of water in silence. Evergreens lined both banks, and the sound of babbling water was a beautiful soundtrack.

"Look out!" Denison yelled, ruining the moment as he leapt between Riley and Diem. He exploded into a bear just before he hit the water.

The giant splash that followed got them all.

"I just saw Denison's butt-cheeks," Riley complained.

"Girl, get used to it," Danielle said sympathetically. "Shifters have no reservations about nudity, and the boys haven't had a chance to Change together in a while. You're going to see all kinds of butt-cheeks this trip. Swinging dicks, too. Give it a few hours, and it won't be uncomfortable for you anymore. They literally don't care, so it's hard to keep up that level of embarrassment for long. Trust me.

They look the same to me naked as clothed now."

"Little nudists," Riley murmured, shocked as Brighton and Kellen began shucking their clothes. "Will you Change, too?" she asked Drew, suddenly excited by the thought of meeting his bear when the animal wasn't raging.

Drew hesitated, eyes on the others as they jumped into the water one by one. "I don't know."

"I want to see him. And maybe this is a good time for your bear to be with the others, when there's no tension."

"Yeah, you're right." His words sounded confident, but his blond brows were still knitted with concern.

With an encouraging smile, Riley tugged on his hand and led him into a grove of lodgepole pines. "I'll help."

He held still with a sexy smirk on his face while she pulled at the fly of his jeans. "You're gonna help me get off?"

"No, I'm going to help you get undressed. Stop fondling me," she said with a giggle, swatting away his wandering hand. "People will see us."

"It'll be erotic. Race to come and try not to get

caught."

"Stop it," she muttered, tugging his sweater over his head.

"Let's go into those bushes, and you can sit on my face."

"Drew! Shut your filthy mouth." She bit back her smile because the man didn't need the encouragement. "And I'm pretty sure you are the first man who has ever said that combination of words."

"Let's wander off in the woods and fuck like ferrets."

"Drew." She gave him dead eyes.

Sidling closer, he gripped her hips and waggled his eyebrows. "Let's scamper off into these here trees and bang like bears."

With a put-upon sigh, she quit trying to take his pants off. "Or we can make whoopee like walruses."

Drew snorted and tucked a wayward strand of her short hair behind her ear. "You're fun."

She glowed under his compliment. She hadn't felt like much fun over the past couple of years, but here, with him, she was opening up like a spring flower. "We can make coitus like caterpillars. Oh," she said, wincing. "That one's weird."

"Do caterpillars do it from behind or missionary." He frowned and canted his head. "Or is it the butterflies that hump? Humping butterflies?"

"Not sexy."

"Nah, they'd be so cute, like..." Drew put his pointer fingers on top of each other and wiggled them around, then said, "Oooh," in a squeaky, high-pitched voice.

"Turn into a bear, gosh dangit."

"Bossy," he accused.

"You like it."

"I love it," he growled out, nipping at her neck.

He kicked out of his pants and backed away a few paces. His eyes were already lightening to that icy color she'd grown to adore. He pushed a quick huff of air out of his lungs, then hunched inward for a split second before an enormous grizzly burst from his skin. The Change was instantaneous, and a smattering of pops echoed off the trees.

His fur was a grayish color, soft looking from here, and his nose was pitch black, contrasting with the stark white teeth she could see behind his curled lip.

Even on all fours, he was taller than her at the

muscular hump behind his shoulder blades. If he stood on his hind legs, he'd tower over her like an ancient oak tree.

She should've been terrified to be around such an enormous, dangerous animal. Hell, his paws were bigger than her head, and his claws were each like black, curved daggers. But she could still see some of the Ashe Crew in their bear forms, splashing around in the river like kids on summer vacation. It was hard to be intimidated, knowing their human sides still ruled their logic.

And Drew was looking at her with such uncertainty, as if he was afraid of her reaction.

"Can I touch you?" she asked.

Drew approached slowly and rested his head gently against her arm. With the other, she ran her fingers through the coarse fur behind his ear. She slipped her arms around his neck and hugged him to her, burying her face in his scruff. He smelled like animal, earth, and something familiar that she was helpless to identify with her weakened human senses. When at last she eased away, Diem was staring at them with tears in her big whiskey-colored eyes, her hands clasped in front of her mouth as if she'd just seen the ending to a romantic movie.

Drew turned but waited for Riley with questioning eyes. She twined her fingers into the fur over his ribcage and walked alongside him until they reached the water's edge. Denison was headed their way in a determined doggy-paddle, so wise woman she was, Riley backed away and avoided another helping of river water splashed across her clothes. Already she was going to have to change her wet jeans from Denison's first grizzly-sized cannonball.

As she stepped back beside Diem, Riley watched the bears on the bank and in the river. She watched the giant falcon as Skyler took off into the air again. Brooke was laughing and chasing little Wyatt around while Kellen unloaded the backs of the trucks. And it struck her that she belonged. No one was staring at her stomach, wondering why there wasn't a ring on her finger, or judging her based on the trial or what had happened last night with Seamus. She was caught up in this simple existence with these people who were wiggling their way into her heart.

Diem draped her arm across Riley's shoulders and rested the side of her head against her temple. "You feel it?"

Riley knew what she meant. Diem had been right about the magic, but it wasn't contained in the trailer park. The magic was in these people.

"Yeah," she whispered, afraid to break the enchantment of the moment. "I really do."

THIRTEEN

Haydan had created a new drinking game. Each time anyone said "dragon," they took a swig. Boxed wine and beer seemed to be the go-to libations of the raucous group, while Riley was already on her second glass of ice water. Now, it might've sounded easy to not say "dragon," but apparently it was nearly impossible for Kellen.

And now even Brighton was slurring his whisper.

Riley couldn't stop laughing, and at this point, her cheeks hurt from grinning. She swallowed another bite of steak and shook her head in disbelief that anything could be this good outside of a dream. "Why does food cooked over an open fire taste so much better than food cooked in a kitchen?"

"Have you never had a cookout before?" Haydan asked, tearing into a package of marshmallows. He was the most intimidating looking man of the group with his shaved head and a tattoo across his neck and down one arm. He was wearing a pair of jeans and no shirt, as if the cold didn't affect him at all. But when she'd gotten the chance to talk to him throughout the day, he had been nothing but polite. He'd even made her plate before anyone else had filled theirs.

"This is my first cookout ever. Even when I've eaten s'mores before, I made them in the microwave."

"Nooo," Denison drawled out. "That's not right. S'mores are made for open fires."

"Yeah, but Denny's a bit of a pyro," Danielle said, tweaking his cheek with her fingers.

Denison snapped his teeth at her with a hungry look that made Riley blush for witnessing the intimate moment between them.

From behind her, Drew chuckled warmly at their antics. He was resting against a log he'd dragged by the fire, and Riley was encased warm and safe between his legs, leaning back against his chest. He was absently stroking her belly, chasing Harper's movement as the firelight threw a golden glow across her.

Today had been amazing. Drew had stayed a bear for a couple of hours, while she, Danielle, Diem, and Kellen had pitched the tents. She'd been a bit lost on the first one, but apparently Danielle was some super-outdoorsy environmentalist who wrestled tents on the regular, and she had Riley whooped into shape in no time. It was satisfying working with them to get camp set up instead of sitting around wondering how she could help.

When the bears had Changed back, they'd all gone on a hike through the woods and witnessed the most breathtaking mountain views. She'd never seen anything like this place. Sure, the pine beetles had killed off a lot of the trees, but it was still beautiful wilderness. Drew had doted on her, helping her up, and resting with her when she was tired. He even carried her for a while when her feet began to swell and her hiking boots felt too tight. He'd steadied her on the hike, his touch never far away, as if he anticipated her needs. And he wasn't the only one.

The men here were all like that. Every one of them treated the women like equals, but rushed to help if they ever asked.

Lunch had been eaten on the trail, and all along, Danielle had collected plants and late season flowers into a little notebook she carried with her, while the others joked constantly in that easy banter that only came when people truly enjoyed spending time with each other.

And now here they were as the sun sank behind the mountains and the first stars twinkled back at her. Being here with the Ashe Crew, cuddled against Drew—her Drew—everything just felt right in the world. Seamus was in transit back to Minneapolis thanks to the statements and pictures the crew had taken, Harper was safe and dancing around in her tummy, and this burly crew of bear shifters and their mates were treating her like she was one of them. She'd never fit into a place so completely. She'd always been the puzzle piece with the odd shape, and now she'd finally found her match.

"You gonna eat the rest of that?" Denison asked.

"Dude," Drew muttered, throwing a bean from Riley's plate at him across the fire. "You don't take food from a pregnant lady."

Kellen looked troubled beside Denny. "That's no way to treat the Vessel of the Dragon."

"Drink!" Drew called out.

Snickering ensued as the crew scrambled for their beers and Dixie cups of boxed wine.

"This is a stupid game," Kellen groused, but his mate, Skyler, bumped his shoulder, and a tiny smile curved his lips.

"I am actually full," Riley conceded, handing Diem her plate to pass around the circle to Denison.

"You didn't eat much," Diem said with a frown as she took the metal plate, still warm from dinner. "Are you feeling all right?"

"Oh, fine. I just don't have that much room in my stomach anymore. Harper makes it hard to eat a lot in one sitting." Though tonight she'd lost a bit of her appetite, too. Perhaps from all the excitement of the day or something. Come to think of it, she was a bit worn out from the hike and losing steam quickly, as well. She was just feeling a bit...strange. "I think I'm going to turn in early."

Brighton stopped plucking lazy notes on an old guitar and rasped out, "What? No, stay."

"No, I remember those days," Brooke said, rocking her sleeping boy gently in her arms. "Pregnancy exhaustion is no joke."

"We'll try to keep quiet if you want to take the farthest tent over there," Tagan said from behind his wife and son.

"Thanks. And don't worry about keeping quiet. I don't think anything will keep me awake tonight." Drew pushed her upward like she weighed nothing, then stood himself.

"Night," he murmured, following behind her.

"Oh, no, I feel bad. You can stay if you want," she said, snuggling against his chest.

"Yeah, Drew, stay," Haydan said through a grin. "You're finally not being an asshole. We've missed the fun you."

"Shut it," he muttered, throwing his friend the finger over his shoulder and leading Riley toward the row of tents. "And don't worry about taking me from our friends. It's not like I don't see them every day. I want to be with you, and if I can't sleep, I'll go back to the fire after you're out for the night."

"Okay, deal." That compromise did make her feel a lot better.

She got a little queasy when she brushed her teeth with Drew by the river. He rubbed her back and looked worried. The day had definitely taken its toll on her, but she wasn't going to regret the trip. This had been one of the best times of her life.

Sinking into the air mattress in the tent, she exhaled a relieved sigh as she watched Drew pull his sweater over his head. His arms and abs flexed with the movement in the artificial light the lantern threw. The claw mark Bruiser had given him that first day was nothing more than a light pink mark that would probably go away in a couple of days. It reminded her of how different Bear was today than when he'd attacked his friend.

"Come snuggle me," she said as he pulled a leather necklace from his neck. He tossed it onto his pile of clothes in the corner and kicked out of his boots.

"Yes, ma'am," he said softly, a tender smile in his voice.

It was chilly out, but the blanket over them was thick and Drew was roughly the temperature of the sun, so the gooseflesh disappeared from her skin in no time.

"Hey," he said, settling behind her and pulling her against his chest. "I liked watching you with the crew today. You fit with us."

She smiled at the gray nylon tent wall as the compliment settled over her.

"And I like that you say what you mean and don't get intimidated around everyone. It can be overwhelming. Everly had trouble adjusting at first."

Riley could see that. Everly was Brighton's mate and was naturally shy. It would be easy to get lost in a group with such big personalities.

"Well, I liked the way you let me see your bear today and how you took care of me without coddling me. I imagine that's a difficult balance with your animal instincts."

He chuckled deep in his chest, the sound vibrating against her back. "You have no idea."

"Drew?" she asked, flopping over. She'd meant for it to be graceful and swift, but instead she probably resembled a tuna fish on dry land. Damn air mattress.

He laughed and tried to help, but it took a ridiculously long time to get situated facing him.

"What?" he asked, practically wheezing with

amusement.

"I was just going to say, before I ruined the moment with my floundering, that I like you."

"Oh," he said, trying to contain his laughter. "That's very serious. You like me."

"I do, and stop your smirking. I like you, and I think we should be exclusive." For the next two weeks, but she banished the sad thoughts. There was no room for that in this tent.

Drew reached over and turned off the lantern, casting them both in shadow. "Oh, so I should stop banging my other girlfriends?"

"I'm being serious. And don't talk about other girlfriends. It makes me feel all angry and want to claw you."

"Mmm," he growled. "Dangerous little human, there's no need to claw me. I was yours from the moment I looked into your eyes." He stroked her short hair out of her face and cupped the back of her head. With a lingering kiss to her forehead, he murmured, "Now sleep. You had me worried tonight."

Riley was already well on her way, all tucked up close to Drew and feeling safe. Outside, Brighton and Denison were playing a slow country song, and in the woods beyond, the crickets were singing along. Her eyes grew heavier as she inhaled Drew's scent, and she clenched her fist against his chest.

And in the moment right as she drifted off, she could've sworn she heard him whisper, "I love you."

****

Riley gasped and sat straight up.

"What's wrong?" Drew asked in an alarmed voice in the dark.

"I don't know," she rushed out. She felt panicked and strange, but couldn't put her finger on why. If it had been a noise outside, Drew would've woken up first. He was the lightest sleeper she'd ever met.

"You smell different," he said low.

"I'm wet. Oh my God, am I bleeding?"

"No, no, not blood. It doesn't smell like iron. Shit." Drew fumbled with the lantern in the dark.

She squinted blindly when he turned it on.

"I'm peeing!" Horror filled her as wetness spread down the legs of her charcoal-colored cotton pajama pants.

"It's not pee," Drew murmured, eyes wide as he stared at her thighs. "I think your water broke."

"No," she whispered, devastation clogging her

throat. "I was supposed to have two more weeks."

"Wait here. I'm going to get help." Drew rocketed out of bed and didn't even bother putting his boots or shirt on before he disappeared through the tent flap and into the night.

She was leaking steadily now with tiny gushes when she moved, like a dam breaking. *Not now! Harper girl, I'm supposed to have two more weeks here with these people...with him.*

Tears burned her eyes, and this time, she didn't hold them back.

Diem threw open the door of the tent, looking worried and disheveled. Tagan and Bruiser followed, then Brooke, and it was getting crowded in the four-person-sleeper.

Tagan's nostrils flared. "Yeah, it's your water. Smells like Brooke's did."

Diem knelt down and pressed her hand on Riley's tummy, her eyes brimming with moisture. "We're going to have a baby today."

Happiness surged through Riley. She was going to make Diem and Bruiser's dreams come true today. She was going to make the guilt of what Seamus had done easier to bear.

Then sadness washed over her just as quickly. Her time here would be at an end. She couldn't be here and watch Diem and Bruiser raise the child that had stolen her heart. Couldn't stand by and watch them love her and kiss her, hold her hand, push her in the swing, take her to preschool. Someday she would have that with a child of her own, but her heart didn't see anything but Harper right now.

Riley's emotions were wrecked as she helped them pack her few belongings into her backpack. Everyone spoke in hushed, excited tones, but she didn't understand the words that were coming from them. It was all a rush, strands of conversation that blurred together as her mind raced on and on.

Drew, Drew, Drew, her Drew. He would be hurt when she left. Why had she let this get so far? *Because you thought you had weeks, not hours, with him.*

A sob filled her throat as she followed the others out of the tent and into the night.

FOURTEEN

Damon Daye's house was so cold.

The midwife requested the heater be turned up to someone outside the door.

Clean towels, clean linens, everything in white. Why white? Why not black to hide the stains better?

Screaming, curling into herself, agony.

She'd left Drew at the door. The separation had already begun.

Diem held her hand tight, but the room was a blur.

Sweat, effort, pain.

Push, rest, push, rest, forever and ever.

It would never end.

But then it did.

A baby's cry.

"It's a girl," the midwife said in a proud voice.

Eyes closed. Keep them closed. Don't look at her, or you'll never be okay.

"Do you want to see her?" Diem, so sweet. So caring about her feelings.

This was her moment, though. Diem had her daughter.

"Can you take her away?"

"Riley—"

Ragged whisper. "Please?"

Harper's cries faded. Door clicked closed.

Midwife looked sad as sobs wracked Riley's body.

It wasn't supposed to be like this.

She was supposed to feel relief.

This was supposed to be her redemption.

So why did it suddenly feel like she'd just lost everything?

FIFTEEN

The nurse hugged her shoulders and the midwife, Dora, followed.

It was the older woman's sad smile that brought a sigh of resignation from Riley's lips. "What?"

"I just don't want you to rush and do anything you'll regret, dear. It's okay to have feelings about these things, you know?"

She did know. She'd been trying desperately to keep her well of feelings from overflowing completely and ruining Diem and Bruiser's moment. "I'll be fine. I'll deal with everything better if I'm not right in the thick of it like I am here."

"Okay." She and the nurse headed for the door, but Dora turned back to Riley before she left. "You know, Riley, you fit in the shifter world. You've slipped in here and found your place seamlessly. It's been wonderful to watch you and Diem's relationship grow over the last few days here. Don't take friendship like that for granted."

"I won't. I'm going to call her the second I get home." Emotion made her words come out too airy, so she stopped talking and gave Dora a little wave.

Puffing air out of her cheeks, she fingered a small, gold heart necklace Damon had given her as a push present. On the front, her initial was engraved, while on the back, there was a cursive *H* for Harper with the baby's birthstone jewel beside it—a tiny opal. She would wear it every day for always to remember the little girl she'd protected and loved. The little dragon, or bear, that owned her heart.

Damon knocked softly on the doorframe. Dressed impeccably, as always, he stood with his elbow extended. He'd already asked her to stay. It had been so hard telling everyone no, especially since she hadn't been able to put into words the reasons she couldn't stay. No one would understand.

Mason had already taken her bag down to the car while Dora and the nurse had checked her one last time to approve her for travel, but now it was time to leave this place and begin to heal.

Damon waved goodbye from his front porch as Mason drove her away. The man was always stoic, but today he seemed to be wrestling with his emotions. He kept swallowing hard as she waved back to him.

Heart in her throat, she turned around and cradled her duffle bag over her now-empty stomach like a comfort blanket.

She was about to leave Diem and Damon and Bruiser.

She was about to leave the Ashe Crew and the mountains she'd fallen in love with.

She was about to leave Drew.

The ache in her chest burned brighter, and she swallowed a sob so she wouldn't catch Mason's attention. Already, he'd cast her a few concerned looks in the rearview.

Scooting over to the window, she bit her thumbnail and tried to blink her tears back. She couldn't say goodbye to Drew or to the others. She'd always been shit at goodbyes and wouldn't ever leave if she had to go through something so traumatic. This was for the best, she told herself, as she had a hundred times already. A clean break would be easier for everyone.

On and on they drove as, outside the window, evergreens passed in a muddy patchwork of greens and browns. The sky was overcast with fast moving, rain-heavy clouds, creating a dark ambiance that fit her mood. They passed the switchback and the landing. The long arms of the metal equipment stood frozen in the air, as if in mid-chore when the Ashe Crew had called it a day.

She searched for Drew's truck, but the dirt parking area was completely empty.

"When I was your age, I fell in love with a woman," Mason said.

Riley frowned and looked at him through the rearview mirror. His eyes had gone emotional as the road passed beneath the tires of the dark Town Car.

"Do you know what I am, Riley? What kind of shifter?"

"Drew told me you are a boar shifter. Not a pig, but one of those huge Russian boars with the long tusks."

"Yes. And in my culture, the males sometimes take two or three mates in a lifetime. We're not monogamous by nature, but I was. I am. My mate was human, and she died after we'd been paired for only two years."

"Oh no, Mason. I'm so sorry."

He shook his head slowly and told her, "Don't apologize for things that aren't your fault, Riley. Not ever. I got two beautiful years with my Esmerelda. Two years of memories that will last a lifetime because there will never be another for me."

Unease filled her as the Asheland Mobile Park came into view. "Why are you telling me this?"

"Because I believe in love and not wasting it."

"I don't understand."

Mason didn't answer but instead pulled through the back entrance of the trailer park and pulled the car to a stop in the middle of the street.

He turned in the driver's seat, sadness pooling in his dark eyes. "I'm sorry. I know you didn't want to say goodbye, but I can't take you out of here without you hearing what they have to say."

"What?" she asked in a panicked voice as her

door opened.

Drew stood there, one arm behind his back in a formal gesture she'd never seen him do, the other hand outstretched to her. His chin was lifted high, and hurt was etched in every beautifully masculine facet of his face.

She couldn't breathe.

Be brave.

Slipping her hand in his, she allowed him to help her out. Tenderly, she stepped out of the car to face the Ashe Crew. Every one of them were gathered in a half-circle in front of her—everyone but Diem and Bruiser.

"I know you're leaving," Drew said quietly. "I knew it from the moment you looked at me with your heart in your eyes when you went into that room to have Harper. I knew I'd lost you, and it gutted me. I can't live with myself and with your decision unless I try, though, Riley. You're it for me. My mate, my better half, the part of my soul I thought had gone dark before I met you. You're my light." His voice hitched, and he cleared his throat and rested his hands on his hips, staring at her helplessly before he continued. "I've talked to Tagan and the others. I'll leave this place for you. I understand the reasons you don't want to be here, and they revolve around Harper and the pain of giving up a child who you love so completely. I'll come with you if you'll have me, Riley."

"You'd leave all this?" she asked in a wrecked voice. She gestured to the mountains and to the Ashe Crew. "You'd leave them and the life you've built here. For me?"

"In a heartbeat. You're my mate." He said it with a tiny shake of his head, as if that should've been obvious.

"I can't ask you to leave your crew," she whispered. "I can't."

"Okay, then there is someone you need to meet."

Diem cut through the crowd, holding Harper wrapped in a fuzzy white blanket. Bruiser followed his mate, his dark eyes steady on Riley.

"No," Riley said thickly, shaking her head. She squeezed her eyes tightly shut, and two warm tears slipped down her cheeks. "I told you I can't see her."

Something warm and soft bumped against Riley's chest.

"Hold the daughter you gave us," Diem said,

sniffling.

Riley cradled her in her arms, but refused to look. She couldn't. Her heart would break if she did.

"Mate," Drew said in a deep, thick voice. "Open your eyes and see what you've given to us."

A sob escaped Riley as she cracked her eyes open and looked down at the baby she'd grown and protected. At the tiny baby she'd given birth to. Riley gasped at her beauty. Perfect little nose and ears. A crop of brunette hair like her father's and puckered pink lips. It was her eyes that stunned Riley to stillness, though. One of Harper's eyes was a soft brown, the color of Diem's, and one was blue with a long, reptilian pupil.

"She doesn't need to have her first Change for us to know what she is," Bruiser said in a proud voice. "You have given us the last-born dragon, our little Harper girl."

"Vessel of the Dragon," Kellen said, kneeling.

"Vessel of the Dragon, Brighton rasped out past his ruined vocal chords, following Kellen to his knees in the dirt.

"Vessel of the Dragon," the others repeated, doing the same until every last member of the Ashe

Crew was kneeling in front of her except Diem, who hugged her shoulders tightly.

"You have it in your head how it will be, living here while Bruiser and I raise Harper," Diem said in a voice as soft as a breath. "It's complicated, and emotions are running high, but I want you to know before you make the decision to go or stay that it doesn't have to be how you imagine. It takes a crew to raise a cub, Riley. Every one of us has a part in bringing Wyatt up, and now every member will play a role in raising Harper. You can be a part of that if you want. I know it's not a conventional way to do this, but you feel important. For Drew and for the rest of us. I want Harper to grow up knowing you and knowing the sacrifice you made to give her to us."

Riley hugged Harper closer, inhaling the sweet baby scent of her hair as another pair of tears slipped down her face.

"Drew will be broken without you," Diem said, resting her head against Riley's. "The rest of us will be, too. Stay."

Harper blinked slowly, and her pupils, both human and dragon, contracted, then dilated to normal again. So beautiful. So perfect.

Riley couldn't leave now if she tried. Diem was right. Things didn't have to be the way she imagined as long as everyone was willing. She wasn't being kicked out of Harper's life. She was being invited to take part in it. To watch her grow up and help guide her into the strong woman she knew her real parents would raise her to be.

She could stay here with Drew and be happy and cared for.

She could stay with her friends.

Riley imagined it now, living here, refurbishing furniture and having her own booth at the market in town on the weekends. Living with the man she loved and someday perhaps having a cub of their own. Learning what it would be like to really fit into a place—to belong. If she stayed, she would get to see Drew's face when he saw the headstone she'd ordered for his mother's grave—the white one with the ducks carved into it.

She could be one of the Ashe Crew if she could only force the words past her tightening vocal cords.

Looking at Harper, then at Drew, whose slow-forming crooked smile said the answer was already written all over her face.

"I'll stay," she whispered.

Drew pulled her in close, kissed her lips before she was pulled away into embrace after embrace. Her mate watched her with such adoration as she was passed through the crew. She couldn't keep her eyes from him and that easy, happy smile. That hadn't existed when she'd first met him.

She handed Harper back to her mother and smiled at the woman who had changed Riley's stars with a simple letter pleading for a surrogate.

Riley wrapped her arms around Drew's waist and rested against his chest as his heartbeat drummed steadily against her cheek. "I'll need a workshop," she said.

He chuckled. "Negotiations already. Woman, you can have whatever you want."

"And you can have all of me," she said, looking up into his blue-flame eyes. Pushing up on her tiptoes, she placed her lips near his ear and whispered, "I heard what you said when I was falling asleep in the tent."

Easing back, he said, "Yeah? I do. And?"

"And I love you, too."

The smile on his face faltered and returned

slowly. "Riley, you're not just the Vessel of the Dragon anymore. Now, you're a part of the Ashe Crew." He kissed her lips softly, then rested his forehead on hers. "Welcome home."

WOODSMAN WEREBEAR

Want More of the Saw Bears?

The Complete Series is Available Now

Other books in this series:

Lumberjack Werebear
(Saw Bears, Book 1)

Woodcutter Werebear
(Saw Bears, Book 2)

Timberman Werebear
(Saw Bears, Book 3)

Sawman Werebear
(Saw Bears, Book 4)

Axman Werebear
(Saw Bears, Book 5)

Lumberman Werebear
(Saw Bears, Book 7)

About the Author

T.S. Joyce is devoted to bringing hot shifter romances to readers. Hungry alpha males are her calling card, and the wilder the men, the more she'll make them pour their hearts out. She werebear swears there'll be no swooning heroines in her books. It takes tough-as-nails women to handle her shifters.

Experienced at handling an alpha male of her own, she lives in a tiny town, outside of a tiny city, and devotes her life to writing big stories. Foodie, wolf whisperer, ninja, thief of tiny bottles of awesome smelling hotel shampoo, nap connoisseur, movie fanatic, and zombie slayer, and most of this bio is true.

Bear Shifters? Check

Smoldering Alpha Hotness? Double Check

Sexy Scenes? Fasten up your girdles, ladies and gents, it's gonna to be a wild ride.

For more information on T. S. Joyce's work,
visit her website at
www.tsjoyce.com

Made in the USA
San Bernardino, CA
07 July 2017